SUZANNA

SUZANNA

A Romance of Early California

HARRY SINCLAIR DRAGO

M. EVANS
Essex, Connecticut

Published by M. Evans
An imprint of The Globe Pequot Publishing Group, Inc.
64 South Main Street
Essex, CT 06426
www.globepequot.com

British Library Cataloguing in Publication Information Available

Library of Congress Cataloging-in-Publication Data

Library of Congress Control Number: 2014942914
ISBN: 978-1-59077-412-0 (pbk. : alk. paper)
ISBN: 978-1-59077-413-7 (electronic)

CONTENTS

CONTENTS

SUZANNA
A Romance of Early California

SUZANNA

CHAPTER I

THE KING'S HIGHWAY

IT was high-noon. Heat waves danced across the floor of the arid, sunburnt valley. The brown California hills, broken, irregular, arose in the distance to bar the way. The year was 1835, and summer so far gone that the young, tufted mountain quail were flying.

Stretching away across the long desert leagues, white with its own dust, wound *El Camino Real*— the King's highway—a well-worn trail at best, for all its high-sounding title. And yet, with perseverance, it won through deserts and over mighty ranges, circled mountain torrents or bridged chasms. Weeks and weeks away to the south and east it took you; but eventually one arrived in Mexico City, then the flower of the Americas.

Where the road dipped down into this wide valley was but the starting point of that long trek southward. For, only some ten leagues behind those low hills to the north, lay Monterey.

Wealth untold flowed back and forth over this highway. Doughty men-at-arms, ladies of surpassing beauty, humble friars, coarse ruffians and better mannered banditti suffered each in turn, or prospered, upon its bosom. From governor-general and high dignitaries of church to poorest Indian neophyte, not one but whose eyes turned from time to time to *El Camino Real.* It was much more than an artery of trade. For California, it was the source of news; the producer of revenue; the means by which the children of the *conquistadores* caught the pulse of the land of their fathers: also—because of the coarse ruffians and their more gently mannered brothers by profession—it became the abiding place of danger.

But on this day, however, neither man nor beast appeared to break the somnolent spell of the torrid noon-time. One gazed in vain across the valley for sight of moving thing. Rabbits and coyotes had long since taken to the hills and the shade of the chamiso and manzanita. Only to the north did the eye catch the stir of living object,—a giant vulture, wheeling lazily in the cloudless sky.

Round and round the grisly thing circled, disdaining to come to earth. Suddenly, then, it straightened its wings and rose in sweeping rushes until it was but a speck in the heavens. Five minutes later a small dust-cloud appeared above the pass where the road cut through the hills. The little cloud grew as it advanced. The cavalcade of mules and horses which caused it quickly came into view.

Outriders rode ahead; armed horsemen brought up the rear. Between these guards rode some four or five men. Immediately behind them thundered an eight-mule-team pulling a heavily wheeled wagon.

Once free of the pass, the little company closed up. Foam dripped from the muzzles of their mounts. The youthful leader held up his hand and the party slackened its pace.

The captain of the cavalcade was hardly more than a boy, for all that he gave his orders with a fine sense of authority. He voiced a warm, carefree laugh as he sheathed his blade and lowered the hammers of his muzzle-loading pistol.

"Safe!" he cried, turning toward the white-faced young man who rode at his side. "Bah, Miguel, you've no heart for danger. You and your books,—look to yourself, man; you're white of face. Come, let's have a smile."

The student colored and swallowed heavily under this banter; but he made no attempt to do as he was bidden.

"Do not ask me to smile, Ramon, not after this mad ride," he muttered. "Time to talk of smiling when we've come safely through yonder pass. Pérez knows that the smuggler is at anchor in the bay, and that there will be wagons coming back to the ranchos with goods. Don't expect him to overlook such an opportunity."

Ramon's eyes snapped with good-natured merriment. "*Oyez!*" he cried aloud. "Hear—hear! And did you not say the same thing as we approached this pass in back of us? You have seen Pérez under every clump of manzanita since we quitted Monterey. Indeed you are the true son of a lawyer. God pity poor Pérez if he is ever brought up before you."

Miguel threw up his head at this. "Fine talk you make of pity for him."

"And why not?" the aggravating Ramon demanded. "He is a professional man the same as yourself. You work with the law; he without it. What's the difference,—it's only a matter of choice. You will grow rich; poor Pérez will lose his head. The pity all belongs to him."

"H'm," the young lawyer snorted. "And you mean it—well I know you do. I half wish your abused bandit stops us. The man has robbed and murdered his way to Mexico City and back."

"Of course. The man is a success. But he only robs and kills the rich"—with a shrug of the shoulders—"the rich can stand it."

"You will be fair meat, then," Miguel retorted hotly.

His words brought a grin to Ramon's face. They understood each other very well, indeed. And, although they were of different castes, and the family of one served the other, the impress of this new country had already set to work a spirit of broadness never known in ancient *Castilla*.

"Indeed, what a sweet plum you would be for friend Pérez," Miguel went on. "The son of the richest, caught—captured—led away into the hills. Why, he would bleed your father's purse until it was as impoverished as my own family's."

"Captured?" Ramon echoed. "But I hold my-self no coward—and friend Pérez—by all accounts —is no poltroon, either. Why talk of capture? We may meet; but one will not run the other off."

"We shall see," his friend replied glumly. "Things have come to a pretty pass when a man may not set forth without fear of his life. Conditions go from bad to worse. We are a nation of law-breakers to-day."

"Oh, *muchachito*, you moralizing—you who have this day purchased contraband goods—cloth-ing, shoes and what not—from a smuggler? Un-less my eyes have failed me, I saw the advocate-general himself aboard ship haggling over the price of a piece of silk. And our neighbors,—our rich, haughty grandees—were they not there, too? And yet, you turn up your nose at poor Pérez. I tell you, it is each man for himself. Why should we pay a hundred per cent tax to Mexico? We are not pawns. Pérez, now, has some claim on us. He, at least, spends his gains in our cities."

The young lawyer made a wry face as Ramon went on. The boy's talk was heretical, treason-able; but it was only a fair sample of what one heard on every side. The days of peace and plenty were, apparently, over. Mexico had granted California a constitution; with it had come a new order of things. Men of affairs in the colony were wondering already if they had moved in the right direction. Taxes had increased by leaps and bounds; civil law had become a jest; and worst of all, the soldiers, who had been sent in answer to urgent appeals for protection of some sort, were convicts, and often a greater source of evil than the bandits whom they were supposed to suppress.

The state was being torn apart with jealousies of one sort and another. The wealthy families of the south were insisting that the capital be removed from Monterey to Los Angeles. And Mexico, starvation poor from her war with Spain, was unable to pay the officers of her army. Revolts followed; sectional leaders appeared, eager to enhance their own positions in this time of unrest.

But this strife was directly traceable to, and quite overshadowed by an epoch-marking economic change which was destined to make history. Namely, the secularization of the Indian neophytes.

By one means or another, the decree of the Spanish Cortes, ordering the secularization of the

Mission Indians, had not been published in California until 1821. Since that time it had been a burning topic of conversation. And since it affected every man in the province, it followed, as a matter of course, that revolutions, bitterness and distrust came.

One heard talk of the rights of peons, of Indians, of the sins of the friars—and this in a land where the Franciscans had been supreme for some fifty years, administering the moral, and oftentimes the civil law. They had preached the salvation of the soul; but, intellectually, the mission system had accomplished nothing. The red men were virtually slaves. They worked up wool, tanned hides, prepared tallow and produced the major amount of California's exports. Economically, therefor, the missions were the life and blood of the province. Secularization meant the freeing of the Indians, the restoring to them of the rights of freemen.

Republican ideas were abroad even at this early date in California. This element acclaimed the new order with triumph. The adherents of the Church, on the other hand, viewed it with consternation. It meant the passing of the missions; the loss of a kingly ransom to the papal coffers. In addition to these two parties there was a third, the owners of the great haciendas. Unhappily, this class was divided among itself. The freeing of the Indians was certain to affect them more than it would any other class in the province. Some said that secularization meant cheap labor, and they were for it on that account. Others saw the complete independence of the peon as the next step, should the neophytes be freed. Giving the peon the rights of freemen meant the establishing of him as a social as well as economic equal. The patrician dons revolted at this. Almost equally they resented the heavy hand of the Church, and so, as a compromise, they had espoused the cause of a strict military dictatorship.

The storm of revolt against the old régime was not to be denied, however. The Republicans arose and drove Victoria, the military governor, out of the state. The Franciscans, realizing that the inevitable was about to happen, were plundering and destroying the Mission property. It was the beginning of the end. A new régime, "less mild, less hospitable, less contented; but better tempered for the building of a state" was about to be inaugurated.

It may be surmised from the foregoing that more than one family found its members set against each other. It was so with the House of Gutierrez. Ramon, as can be judged from his talk, was violently Republican. His father, the aged Don Fernando—a true Castillian grandee—a royalist and conservatist without brook or hindrance. Between them there was the clash of unbending wills.

This square jawed, dancing-eyed boy was the son of his father. The head of the House of Gutierrez drew what comfort he could from that thought. Hot words had passed between them already. Young Alvarez, the lawyer's son, had heard the old Castillian threaten to disinherit the boy for his revolutionary ideas. Ramon had smiled.

As the little cavalcade moved across the valley Miguel thought of his friend's ability to smile in the face of such a calamity. He knew that he, for one, would have been among the last to smile. The old order of things quite satisfied young Alvarez. His father had risen to a position of dignity and some affluence through the good graces of his wealthy patrons and the protecting arm of the

Church. Miguel had no ambition beyond striving to emulate his honored sire. Ramon's free speech filled him with resentment. He did not doubt but what time would show his friend the folly of his ways. And Miguel took a secret pleasure in hoping that when enlightenment came it would sink its barb deep enough into Ramon's soul to cure him of his cocksureness about everything in general.

The heat became so intense that the boys' conversation languished. Not until their horses began climbing the benchlands which led up to the pass ahead of them did Miguel speak again. Ramon slept in his saddle, swaying easily from side to side with the motion of his horse. The peon guard lounged along in the rear of the wagon, eyes closed, oblivious to any possible danger.

Miguel glanced ahead to where the cool, inviting shadows of the pass met the eye. Its coolness called to him in vain. He knew there were narrow defiles and sharp turnings beyond which were made to order for the highwayman. Pulling up his horse, he dropped back until he rode beside Ramon.

"*Ea, ea,* brave one," he exclaimed. "Do we go on without taking any precautions whatever?"

Ramon yawned provokingly before replying.

"*Si, muchachito,*" he murmured sleepily, "for your sake we will take every precaution."

Ramon's tone was keenly sarcastic. Miguel's face flushed as he saw him wave his guards ahead with an extravagant gesture.

"Ruiz," the boy heard him address the grim-visaged leader of the peons, "we will wait in the open until you sound the bell,—that is if friend Pérez has not stolen it, clapper and post."

Old Ruiz's lips parted in a mirthless grin. His master jested; but Ruiz had heard tales of bandits carrying off the bells placed in the passes. These bells served the purpose of signals to the wagon-trains waiting in the more open country where they were less liable to be pounced upon. The custom was, as in this instance, to send ahead a mounted guard to explore the defile. When this advance guard had made sure that no foe lay in waiting, the bell would be sounded and the teams would dash through to the succeeding valley.

Ramon caught the look in the old man's eyes. "*Madre de Dios,*" he cried sharply. "We are not

three leagues from the rancho. My father can muster a hundred men, if needs be. Do you think
Pérez or his like court fighting against such odds?
If this senseless talk keeps up we'll all be slinking
about the hacienda itself come another month. Get
off now, and look to it that your own shadow is
not sending you back a sniveling *paisano.*"

Some ten men remained behind with the wagon.
They were mounted, and now formed a circle about
the train. Ramon smiled at Miguel as he saw the
men take their places. "Art satisfied now, reckless one?" he demanded.

Poor Miguel trembled in impotent rage as his
friend baited him on. "I hold my head to better
things than prowess with a sword or accuracy with
a pistol," he answered wrathfully. "Had I but to
please myself, as you so boldly do, I, too, had time
for the graces of a *caballero.* Your Republican
ideals but mock you in shaming me for having held
my nose to books that I might win a place for myself in this new world."

Miguel's words rubbed the smile from Ramon's
face; his eyes filling with contrition as he saw how
deeply his friend was hurt. Impulsively he placed
his hand upon the boy's shoulder. "Forgive me,

compañero," he pleaded. " 'Twas all in fun, and well you know it. Stick to your books say I. Indeed shall we need the like of you. The time comes when we shall be done with Mexico even as we were done with Spain. We shall have our own laws. And you, *jovencito,* shall help to frame them."

"There you go!" Miguel cried with a toss of his head, "tempering your humbleness with farther empty boastings. Your talk is well calculated to lead you to the gibbet, yet. I, for one, would not——" Miguel did not finish his admonition. His keen eyes had caught the movement of Ramon's hand as he reached for his sword. He saw the boy's mouth straighten, his body stiffen; and poor Miguel, dreading to confirm his instant suspicion, turned and gazed at the dark pass ahead of them.

"Virgen santa!" he muttered, the words almost strangling him. Subconsciously he made the sign of the cross.

Four men had broken from cover and were dashing toward the wagon-train. They waved their guns and gave voice to a series of wild, blood-chilling cries as they rode. At first Miguel took them for Ruiz and his guard; but as the boy continued to stare at them, mouth open, eyes wide with terror, the four men became eight, ten, twelve, fourteen!

"Pérez!" broke with a shriek from the boy's lips as understanding flashed within him. "It's Pérez and his band of cut-throats!"

A curse escaped the lips of the youthful leader as he perceived that Miguel spoke the truth. The peon guard was panic stricken already. The boy's mouth straightened as he observed them. He was in for a fight, now, and although his party outnumbered the other, he realized the calibre of his men. That they would stand up before Pérez and fight was not to be hoped for. And yet, as the bandit crew dashed toward him, Ramon determined to resist them.

He found time to ask himself what had happened to Ruiz and his men. Ruiz was too wary to walk into a trap with his eyes open. The boy fumed at his stupidity in having sent his best men ahead. With hope born of desperation, he drew his sword and made ready for the oncoming outlaws.

"Fool!" Miguel cried. "Don't you see that it is Pérez?"

"Croaker, you are right for once! He's ridden

in between Ruiz and us. Well, look to yourself now! Close your ears to those cries; they've driven off more men than his guns ever have."

"But we are only a handful! These peons will not fight. We had best run while we can."

Ramon shook his head slowly. "No," he snarled, his eyes narrowing; disgust for the other's cowardice contorting his mouth. "I stay! Run, you with your rabbit's soul! My father has already called me fool. *Por Dios* he'll not write coward after my name. I am going to fight!"

CHAPTER II

A LADY'S NAME IS MENTIONED

PÉREZ and his band began to circle when they were still some three hundred yards away. It was a well-known Indian maneuver long since adopted by road-agents. It reduced the morale of those at bay to the minimum. Also, it resulted in a surprisingly small loss of life among the attackers.

Ramon hurled orders at his peons as he saw himself being surrounded. The poor devils had no heart for this affair. All of them were supplied with guns and had some minor skill with them; but the boy realized how little he could expect from them as they glanced at him, the whites of their eyes showing, their muscles seemingly atrophied.

"When I give the order," Ramon cried, "you fire. I'll run my blade through the heart of the one who throws down his gun. Ruiz will hear the shooting. If his party has not been captured, he'll come to our aid. Take to the ground, now!"

The mules and horses had been hobbled and

thrown. Using their bodies as a sort of breastwork, the little party crouched behind them and waited.

The wily Pérez stayed the advance of his men when he deemed that their circle had narrowed sufficiently. Without waiting for the order, his men threw themselves to the ground even as their quarry had. Pérez smiled as he viewed the preparations of the besieged.

"Well, Pablo," he said with a grunt of appreciation to his lieutenant, "the boy is no fool. And yet, the cattle he counts on to win his battle will but defeat him. Indeed 'twill take but a little well-placed lead to bring those quickly hobbled mules to their feet. I'll wager my head that when they begin plunging the señor's carbineers will take to their heels. Let's be at it."

The men who rode with Benito Pérez were old hands at this game. A satisfied grin sat upon their leader's face as he watched the effect of the firing which followed. It was as he had foreseen. The improvised hobbles were kicked off as the wounded animals struggled to get to their feet. Once upon all fours, the mules and horses limped or galloped off, leaving the peons exposed to their enemies.

Slow as their mental faculties were, it took Ramon's men no great time to digest the fact that theirs was a most unhappy position, and that it mattered little whether they remained where they were, to be shot down by Pérez and his band, or died by their leader's sword in attempting to escape.

Whatever advantage the scales held inclined in favor of the latter chance. Pérez would most certainly kill them; Don Ramon, on the other hand, might take compassion on them.

Hope springs eternal, and a chance is always a chance whether it falls to the lot of don or peon. Enough that they became obsessed to get themselves elsewhere. A stealthy, calculating look toward their leader and they were off, the music of Pérez's guns to speed them on.

This defection came so quickly that Ramon was left inert for a minute. Pérez saw him get to his feet. The bandit grinned as he heard the boy curse his men for the cowards they were. And then, as he watched, he saw him empty his pistol at the fleeing wretches.

"*Por Dios,* Pablo," Pérez laughed, "see him! There's good stuff in the boy, I tell you, even though his aim is not the best. He'll handle a

sword better than he does a gun. And that other
one, that sniveling clown beneath the wagon—'tis
the lawyer's cub, is it not?"

Pérez chuckled to himself. "Well he trembles,"
he added. "He has the many threats father lawyer
has made upon my head to console him." The
bandit chieftain got to his feet boldly. "Let you
and the others stay back," he ordered. "I'll have
speech with our young knight."

With a dignity that was little short of regal, for
all his barbaric splendor, Pérez strode toward the
wagon. The boy suffered him to approach to
within ten yards of the spot where he stood before
he spoke to him.

Although Ramon had never met the man, he knew
from a hundred descriptions of him that he faced
Pérez. There was a certain swagger to the man,
a sense of poise and conceit which was not lost on
the boy.

A devilish leer to the once handsome mouth, a
light in his eyes as cold as snow-capped mountains, and the sagging cheek muscles of one who
drank too much, were not enough to conceal the
fact that the man had once been a highly promising
gentleman.

The boy had it upon his tongue to stay the other's advance, when Pérez stopped of his own accord. They took stock of each other before either spoke.

Pérez was the first to break silence. "My regards, young sir," he said, accompanying his words with a sweeping gesture of his sombrero. "A thousand pardons for so forcibly ejecting myself upon you; but in truth there is no other way in which the lowly may meet those of high estate. And yet it grieves me to annoy one who is so evidently cut to my own pattern. You do well; but you are young. In time you will learn many things; let the first of them be, not to put trust in peon stock. They are as you have fashioned them——" Perez shook his head. "In your tailoring of them to do as they were bade, you forgot their spirit. You cut and trimmed it along with their bodies. And now—poor devils—they're nought but sheep. But here is too much talk of mice and men. Allow me to present myself—in lieu of trusting friend, I, sir, am Benito Pérez. And you will be——?"

"Well enough you know me, you jesting devil," Ramon answered hotly. "You have either fooled and killed my scouts—or both, for the matter of that; you have seen those bastard peons run to cover like rabbits before a wolf; you know that I face you alone—for that poor wretch beneath the wagon is but a student of books, a helpless creature, of no aid to me in this hour—I am outnumbered, sadly so, and there is no hand to help me but my own; but I would know what you intend."

" 'Tis a brave speech," Pérez declared, not unkindly, "and one to my liking. With things so heavily set against you, it pleases me to hear you make plain talk. I had but to raise my finger to have you bound and on the way to my camp in the hills. The contents of yonder wagon, all unlawful goods I'll swear, fill my eyes with itching curiosity. But even so, I blush to say that I am hard put to think only of contraband. You yourself are so rich a prize that already my fingers are counting the *pesetas* your honorable father would pay to have you returned to him."

"Nay, that you shall not do," the boy exclaimed. "The goods I waive; but you will not have me alive."

"No? And how do you avoid the inevitable?"

"With fair ease, if half that I have heard of you

were true. Only this day have I spoken good words in your defense. Time there was on this continent when men of our blood fought with honor for all. My men have left me alone on the field; you still have yours, but that were a small matter indeed between gentlemen. Man, we are two leaders. Here and now will I do combat with you, and who wins shall go free. If it falls that I am the fortunate one, your men shall raise no hand to stop me. What sayest you to that, friend Pérez?"

For an instant the bandit's eyes lost their coldness. Here indeed was a man! This boy's talk was not the empty boasting of unbearded youth.

"And you so easily hope to win free, eh?" he asked in bantering tones. "No! More like I should run you through at first thrust. More times than I have hairs on my head have I held my life forfeit against my skill with the dancing steel. Men skilled in arms have held me no mean antagonist. Many there have been to say I was unmatched, and though flattery is the coin that circulates in the lives of those who live by the sword and gun, still, I have come safely through, up until now. Your words do you proud; but for all of them, you are only a boy, an untried gamecock. What bids you believe you will leave my bones here to be picked by those hovering buzzards?" Pérez' smile melted to honest good-will as he answered his own question. "Is it that poor Pérez grows old, or that you have heard how the dampness of the hills swells his joints?"

"Your age and ills matter but little to me," the boy said flatly. "I hold neither you nor myself cheaply. But truly, if your skill with the sword matches your cleverness with the tongue, then I had best beware. I offer myself in fair fight to you. An end to this, then,—what is your answer?"

" 'Tis a pity, young cub, but since you will have it, stand ready."

Pérez called in his men. They had not been so far distant but that they had some idea of what went forward here.

"Let no man's hand but mine touch this boy," he ordered. "It will be an honorable affair even though it is far less than a fair one. Should a miracle happen, and he best me, he goes free. But hiding clown, there beneath the wagon, you shall strip and tie upon a mule, and thus send him back all askew to his blatant father. And now, señor, if you are ready, fall to!"

Ramon's blade flashed on the word. Pérez parried without seeming haste, and yet the movement seemed so easy only because of its grace. The bandit's men had formed a circle about the swordsmen, and even the white faced Miguel had moved himself so as to witness this combat.

Crafty Pérez let the younger man circle round and round him, quite content to remain on the defensive, conserving his strength against the propitious moment. But it seemed to his followers that he took no advantage of his first opening, and the thought grew on them that he but played with this boy.

Some thought of this showed in Ramon's eyes, too. It angered him to think he was played with. Still, with surprising good sense, he kept his head free of passion. In and out he continued to dance with the agility of tireless youth.

Pérez met his advances squarely, but time came when he looked to see the boy falter, only to find him as strong as ever. "You yield a stout blade," he cried complimentingly, "for all your foolhardiness. 'Tis easy now to see from where your assurance sprang. Canst parry this?"

And with lightning-like swiftness the man lunged for the boy's heart. Ramon could not get out of his way. A backward step was all he could allow himself at best.

Pérez' eyes narrowed as he saw his opening. The smile was gone from his face and there remained only cupidity, cruelty, and the mirthless grin of the killer. He set himself, ready for his opponent's backward step which should deliver the boy to him.

Too late, he saw that Ramon braced himself where he stood. Rare intelligence had whispered to the boy that retreat would only leave him unbalanced and a fair target. To stand his ground could be no more dangerous. A snap of his wrist altered the direction of his blade, so that it flashed at Pérez' wrist. By the time it fell, the boy's shoulder was behind it.

The older man saw his danger, but there was left him only the chance that his steel would reach the other in time.

A gasp escaped the onlookers, all fair swordsmen themselves. They knew that the decision impended and that it hung upon who should strike first,—a space of time so slight that to call it a second is to exaggerate.

Even with the thought came the answer,—a loud ringing of steel upon steel, their leader's sword broken off short and the boy facing them unscathed.   Remained now but for him to finish his antagonist.

Pablo groaned as understanding flashed upon him; but he made no move to turn the scales.   He was an outlaw with a price on his head, as indeed were his fellows; they were without morals, illiterate, but they had their code.   Pérez, himself, refused to reach for his pistol.   Quixotic?   But such ideas were abroad in 1835.

With the point of his blade resting upon his boot, Ramon stood facing Pérez.   The boy's face was flushed, his brow wet with perspiration.

"Get at your pig sticking," the highwayman thundered.

"Let that remain for butchers.   I am no peon," the boy flung back at him.

"So I perceive," Pérez said tauntingly, "and yet I hear that you are passing fond of one who is."

Hot anger flashed in the boy's eyes at this.

"The ear often hears what the lips would do well not to repeat. Maybe 'twere better I had run you through. Get yourself another blade and I'll pay you in full for those words."

And so they fell to again, the ring of steel against steel sounding as they circled. Pérez no longer stood still, but forced the fighting whenever it was to his liking. The brightly polished blades caught the rays of the scorching sun, until it seemed at times that the men fought with swords of fire.

Minutes fled and still no advantage came to either. Awe, and envy for such skill, shone on the faces of those who watched. They had seen their leader give battle times without number, but not one could remember having seen him maneuver as he did now, and graceful as his foot-work was, it less than matched the nimble agility of this dancing boy.

The crafty Benito saw that he tired the quicker, and that the long battle but served the cause of youth. Hence, he resorted to banter to aid himself.

Ramon, smarting under the man's thinly veiled insinuations, let fly an angry thrust which Pérez avoided and placed to his own advantage by countering dangerously close to the boy's throat.

The bandit's eyes must have mirrored his thought, because the boy gritted his teeth and cursed himself for the fool he had been in thus delivering himself. Two could play at words as well as one! Even Pérez had to smile as he realized that he had tossed away his opening, for although he taunted and abused the boy, Ramon but grinned, and in turn, hurled biting bits of sarcasm and scorn at him.

So, in desperation, Pérez resorted to a dangerous trick. Purposely he made a wide thrust and seemed to lose his footing. Ramon rushed into the trap by lowering his rapier and setting himself for a death blow.

Pérez snapped erect at that, and his sword flashed out with unbelievable swiftness. Ramon divined his mistake when it was too late, but even so, Pérez saw him throw his body away from the piercing blade. That he could escape entirely was impossible.

The next instant came a faint, sucking sound and a spurting stream of blood. The boy's weapon fell to the ground, as with his left hand he reached for his arm where Pérez' blade had passed clean through.

A look of pain distorted the boy's mouth as Pérez pulled free his blade. But with fine fortitude, he faced his conqueror the next instant.

The bandit's eyes wore a strange veil as he stared at the youth before him. "Well," he said gruffly, at last, "the tables are now turned, *jovencito!*"

Ramon bowed his head. "I await your pleasure," he said bravely.

"My pleasure?" the robber questioned. "And do you think to shame me by expecting less than you so lately volunteered?"

"The incidents are not at all the same," the boy averred. "It had been no fight at all had I finished you with your weapon useless to you; but now, no man can say but what we have both done our best. Your ruse was well executed, and I submit with what grace I can to you; but as I said on oath, I shall not be taken prisoner and carried off so that you may mulct my father."

"Rest easy on that score," Pérez said abruptly. "You, Pablo," he called to his lieutenant, "look to the man's wound." Turning back to Ramon he continued: "Your bark is loud, but it is becoming; one that I warm to, for you have proved your worth in the only way that I set store by,—man to man. I have an ill name in this land, and yet I hold that no man, be he son of don or peon, can say that Benito Pérez ever failed to repay a courtesy with lesser coin. You shall go on your way, and your wagon with you; but as a favor, and not as an order, I'll take from you a piece of goods,—no less than a piece of the finest, either. Silk, or a yardage of some rare material such as I know you have purchased for your most august mother. I want it bright, colorful, of surpassing beauty, because it is for one who is surpassingly beautiful. Will you accommodate me?"

Pablo had bound the boy's wound by now, and Ramon, his good nature restored in part, addressed himself to Pérez in a manner fully as grandiloquent as that which the bandit had employed. "The choice rests with you," he said, pointing to the wagon. "The silks are beneath the seat, in a package by themselves."

"A thousand thanks," Pérez grinned impudently. "And it were well not to waste time in the choosing, for here comes your guard at full tilt."

He pointed to the distant pass from which Ruiz and his men now emerged. Suiting his action to his words, Pérez speedily located the package of silks and broke it open. With a sweep of his hand he spread them so that the different pieces were displayed. One, in particular, caught his fancy. Holding it aloft, he turned to Ramon. "A rich mogador!" he exclaimed. "All shot with gorgeous colors,—the very thing!"

"Not being acquainted with the lady," Ramon answered facetiously, "I can not advise you. You, who know her tastes, must decide."

Pérez stopped abruptly in the act of folding the brightly colored silk. "That, I do not," he exclaimed. "Nor, I suspect, does she. Her tempers, now, that were a different matter. For all her airy graces, she is a peon, and take this parting bit of advice,—even in love, a peon is a disappointment."

Pérez swung on to his horse and with a wave of his hand sped away in full cry, his men in hot pursuit.

Miguel crawled out from his hiding place beneath the wagon, his face still working convulsively. He uttered an unintelligible sound as he saw that Pérez had actually gone.   Ramon turned his back on him, in a white rage at the bandit's parting shot.   The taunt had been too thinly veiled to be misunderstood.   There was but one to whom the man could refer; and yet, he had been the first to dignify the affection existing between Ramon and that one by the word love.   Love? The boy smiled at his own question.   Yes, he admitted to himself, it well might be love.   The The word peon, however, had been used to him in this instance with malicious intent.   The thought made Ramon's lips curl venomously.   Damn the hypocrisy of a social system that allowed even a bandit to brand a girl with such a sweeping term of scorn.

"By the Holy Mother, Suzanna!" he muttered aloud.   "That dog shall pay me yet for his loose tongue!"

CHAPTER III

THE HONOR OF THE DONS

Across the San Carmelo hills the semi-tropical sun bathed the adobe buildings which comprised the *caserio* of the *Rancho de Gutierrez*. From bleached earth and sun-baked *caserio* there arose a haze of blinding heat.

It was siesta time, and, no word of Ramon's adventure having reached the rancho, the hacienda slumbered. Except for a collie dog wandering about in search of relief from the noon-time sun; the occasional flutter of a chicken's wings as it burrowed deeper into the cool earth in the shadow of the patio wall; the drone of insects; or the bawling of a calf temporarily estranged from its mother, there were few sounds of life.

The hour dragged on; higher rose the sun, reached its zenith, and then began swinging westward, a copper colored ball of fire.

At last, from across *El Camino Real,* which wound past the *caserio,* the sound of a bell penetrated the sweltering stillness. The ringing of the bell was the signal that the afternoon's work was to start; the daily siesta was over.

But although the summons of the bell had been sudden, the *caserio* awakened with deliberation to resume the day's labors. Neither the master, nor Spanish overseers, appeared to urge haste, and the Mexican peons and Indian laborers, sure of their ground, moved slowly to their appointed tasks. Therefore, a full half-hour elapsed before the rancho settled down to its work.

Facing the large *casa* of Don Fernando and the cluster of small adobes which were occupied by those employed on the rancho, and which comprised the *Caserio de Gutierrez*, stood another group of buildings belonging to the hacienda of one, Señor Don Diego de Sola.

This grouping of the buildings of one rancho in close proximity to those of another was quite the custom and no matter of accident. It afforded a degree of protection against such men as Pérez. Also, it fostered the social life of the province.

Don Diego and his daughter were sojourning in Mexico City at the present, but in their absence the crops were being gathered and the cattle worked in preparation for the fall *rodeo*.

Strong ties bound the houses of Gutierrez and de Sola. In early childhood, young Ramon had been betrothed to Chiquita de Sola, now a proud, beautiful woman. The designing fathers seeing in the alliance the creation of a princely empire over which their heirs should reign.

However worthy such plans, it is all too true that they often go amiss. Fear of such a *contretemps* now filled the heart of Don Fernando.

Presently, from within the casa, there emerged three persons—two gentlemen and a lady—who seated themselves leisurely upon the shaded portico.

The dominating figure of the trio was Don Fernando Gutierrez, tall, somewhat portly, gray-haired and mustached, epitomizing the true Castilian who ruled not only wisely, but well, over California prior and even subsequent to the Mexican war of 1845.

With characteristic Castillian courtesy, he attended the feminine member of the party—his beautiful, patrician wife, the Doña Luz,—meanwhile the other gentleman stood at respectful attention.

All three were properly, if somewhat overly-attired, in the dress of the period. Doña Luz's gown was of silk, with short sleeves and loose waist. From beneath the hem of her skirt peeped the tips of her diminutive red slippers. In her ears were jet-black pendants. Her black, gray-streaked hair was done high on top of her head and surmounted by a great mother-of-pearl comb. Over her head was drawn a large, greenish-colored mantilla of filmy lace.

Doña Luz looked toward her husband expectantly, for this meeting was in the nature of a conference bearing on no less a topic than her son's conduct.

Because of the occasion, Don Fernando had dressed elaborately, and his guest was hardly less resplendent. Each was attired in a fine linen shirt, rich with a profusion of lace and embroidery. The Señor Gutierrez's heavy silk jacket of deepest maroon, amply decorated with "frogs" and buttons, was unbuttoned, a compromise with the weather. His guest wore a jacket also, of lustrous brown equally well decorated. Their pantaloons of black velvet, decorated with rows of vermilion buttons, harmonizing well with the green sash about the waist, left a lot to be desired on this torrid day. Under the pantaloons, and visible through the knee-length slit, were boots of untanned deer-skin.

Satisfied as to the comfort of his wife, Don Fernando waved his guest to a chair, and then seated himself. Without turning, he called in husky tones, "José!" Almost immediately a Mexican *mozo*, or houseboy, appeared in the area-way.

"*Aguardiente*—brandy," commanded the don briefly.

"*Si, señor*," came the soft reply, and the boy disappeared across the patio.

This patio was a rectangular court surrounded on three sides by verandas upon which opened the various rooms that composed the casa. Across the southern end stretched a high wall. In the center of it was an arched door-way through which one passed from the don's patio to that of the servants.

This patio was a veritable garden of beautiful flowers and plants,—roses, geraniums, oleanders and flowering cactus. An acacia tree, in full bloom, adorned one corner, while in another was an arbor of bougainvilla. Caressing each pillar that supported the tile-roofed veranda were vines of one description or another. In the center of the patio was a well, fully fifteen feet in diameter, which supplied the house with water.

Several minutes passed before the servant returned with the brandy. Meanwhile, the three sat silent, gazing out across the garden patio and to the servants' patio beyond.

Worry wreathed the face of the Señor Gutierrez. Nervously, he gnawed the ends of his bristling gray mustache. Doña Luz frowned as she saw her lord's perturbation. Well enough she knew that he would not speak until it so pleased him. Her son's delayed arrival also wore on her. Turning away, she sent her eyes across the fields to where the Santa Cruz mountains lay basking in the sun. For all their brown, barren, forbidding appearance, she loved them. Raised, as she had been, in more urban surroundings than rural California could boast, this queenly woman had missed those niceties of life which would have been hers in a more sheltered land. Long since, she had turned to her flowers and those distant, friendly hills;

and found that California could win her smiles as well as ancient Seville.

José soon reappeared with goblets, brandy and cigars—huge, cylindrical, black. He served with the sureness and precision of a trained servant, and disappeared.

The don and his guest lighted their cigars, then joined the doña in sipping from the old, hammered-silver goblets the deliciously refreshing liqueur.

For several more minutes the don looked reflectively across the patio, puffed at his cigar, and toyed with his goblet. Then turning to his visitor, who was eyeing him curiously, he said:

"Alvarez, you are my attorney; likewise, you are my friend. I have sent for you to advise me."

Alvarez bowed his head. The don thought for a moment, then resumed:

"It is about Ramon."

Alvarez—the boy Miguel's father—feigned his surprise. He had been quite aware of the subject to be discussed, but he was a successful lawyer; and lawyers even in that day found it passing wise to dissemble at times. He largely divided his time between Monterey and the hacienda, so it followed that he had an ear to the ground concerning what went on in the household of Don Fernando.

"Your manner, more than your words, alarms me," he exclaimed. "I hope there is nothing of great moment involved in what you have to say."

"I am sorry," Señor Gutierrez replied, "but it is of the utmost concern to my wife and me. There is no need for me to tell you how I regard mixed marriages, or the store I set by my lineage. I thought that I had impounded my tastes and desires in my son. Lately, however, I have had reasons enough to doubt the truth of that. There has even been talk about the boy, and public gossip needs some foundation of fact to survive. I do not know if in your visits here you have noticed the daughter of Ruiz, the peon."

"But, of course," Alvarez stated, "I remember her as a child about the hacienda."

"I would she had remained a child," Doña Luz said pointedly.

"You echo my own wish," Don Fernando went on. "As a child, Suzanna was an unusual little creature, considering her parentage. When Ruiz' wife died, we naturally took a greater interest in her. It was a fatal mistake. The situation that we face now is of our own making. The girl has developed into a beautiful woman, and I'll own, not without a certain sense of poise and wisdom. But she is a peon. Ramon is man grown, too. The intimacy that existed between them as children was well enough; but we cannot tolerate it now. People are coupling their names together. I know my boy's spirit, and I am at a loss what to do. A heavy hand is the last thing I want to use."

"You don't mean that this affair has progressed to the point of love?" Alvarez asked.

"Not yet. But that it will, is most certain. Their fondness for each other has changed gradually from impersonal friendship and good-fellowship to personal regard; although I am sure that neither realizes that love exists. I should have sent the girl away long since. They have never been separated, except for the two years the boy spent in Spain. I used to laugh to see him trundling her about the hacienda." The don slapped his knee and shook his head. "It's no laughing matter today," he finished mournfully.

A period of silence followed. Alvarez' face wore a well-feigned frown. Don Fernando glanced at him sharply as he sat without replying or offering suggestion. "You know that I cannot talk to Suzanna," the father argued. "To do so would be but to make her aware of the very thing I fear. The same thought holds good with the boy. You have got to suggest something, Alvarez."

"It's an awkward situation," the attorney answered. "You are sure you do not exaggerate it?"

"I suppose we do," Doña Luz observed quietly. "But, we must not forget to mention that Ramon is betrothed to the daughter of Don Diego. The girl and her father are expected home shortly. Ramon is a dutiful son; he knows that he is pledged to wed the daughter of our dear friend and neighbor. I am sure that he has some affection for Chiquita, and that he recognizes the engagement existing between them these many years. When the time arrives for the ceremony, he may forget Suzanna entirely for one who is more beautiful and his equal in culture and blood. Remember, too, Fernando," she went on, turning to her husband, "that Ramon has not seen Chiquita in nearly two years. The girl must have improved wonderfully, and when she comes back from the south with the glamour of the capital fresh upon her she may sweep the boy off his feet."

Don Fernando seemed little impressed by these words.

"You know," the Doña continued, "that in Chiquita's absence Suzanna has been the only personable girl the boy has come in contact with day after day."

"Excepting yourself, my sweetheart," the don complimented her.

"Ah, thou flatterer," the señora murmured, but well pleased nevertheless. "But really, I think we worry too much."

"I cannot help worrying," confessed the don, once again serious. "Something here"—placing his hand over his heart—"tells me that there are difficulties ahead."

"There is an old Spanish proverb, *querido*," the doña replied, "which is, in effect, 'wind, women and fortune soon change.' You do not *know* Suzanna's feelings, and even though they are more than impersonal with respect to our Ramon, some dashing vaquero may come along and woo and win her in a day."

"Ah, would that I were so optimistic!" the don cried feelingly.

"Pardon, señor," murmured the attorney, injecting his suave presence into the conversation. "I feel as the señora feels: that when the time for the wedding arrives Don Ramon will not only be ready to respect your wishes that he marry Don Diego's only child, but eager to. However, to make certain that Suzanna will in no wise interfere with the marriage, I suggest that you send her away for a few years."

"That is impossible," Señor Gutierrez declared. "I——"

"Ah, but it is not, señor," Alvarez interrupted quickly. "She is personable, you say? And possessed of intelligence? Very well,—then why not send her to the Mission at San Luis Bautista, and place her under the care of the good Padre Altado. Under his merciful and guiding hand, Suzanna can receive that which not one out of ten thousand peons have—an education.

"Two years must necessarily elapse before she returns. Meanwhile, Don Ramon will have wed, and—who knows?—have been blessed with a son and heir to the vast estates of Gutierrez and De Sola, which naturally are joined by the wedding."

"Just the thing, Alvarez," Don Fernando exclaimed excitedly. "The girl shall leave within the week. But how shall I inform her that she is going, and the reason for it?"

"Wait for a propitious moment, my friend," Alvarez warned, "then, as though rewarding her for some service, tell her. Surely Ramon will not object. If he is anticipating marriage with her, then he would have a woman of some culture and refinement—something she is not now. Her mental education is of small moment: so few women of to-day—be they daughters of dons or of peons—are interested in aught else than to be able to look their prettiest, to act the coquette at all times, or to out-step their sisters when dancing the *jota*. Therefore, you can impress the fact upon both Ramon and Suzanna that because of her beauty and intelligence, she is to be given an opportunity to compete with her more fortunate sisters. It will be a tactful move, and one that will not commit you in any direction."

"Capital!" Ramon's father cried enthusiastically. "You are a very wise lawyer, my Alvarez. Suzanna shall go to San Luis Bautista!"

"But Ramon," Alvarez warned, "—I should say nothing to him about this matter until you are ready to announce your decision to Suzanna.

Then, if the idea does not please him, he will have no time to plan a counter move."

"Ramon is an obedient son," Doña Luz hurriedly assured the lawyer. "He will not question his father's authority."

"No,—of course not," the attorney answered with a rather forced smile. "But the boy does his own thinking. It is the way of our young men. Ramon had no hand in the Republican coup that sent Victoria out of the state; but from what Miguel tells me, I can see that the boy is Republican; and it is the doctrine of that element to tear down all of our old institutions."

"And small wonder," Don Fernando exclaimed. "If my son is a Republican it is because Mexico administers things so badly, and not because he has turned against the traditions we brought here from Spain. He is nearer right in his beliefs than I would care to have him suspect. But it matters not, Alvarez. He shall not be told until I am ready to speak to the girl. When I announce myself, she will do as I order."

CHAPTER IV

As they talked, a slip of a girl,—small-limbed, small-waisted; but full breasted and muscular for all her size, rode across the servants' patio. Even though she sat astride a sleepy-eyed, flea-bitten burro, her attire the ragged clothes of a peon boy, she was beautiful.

From the crown of her head—partially hidden from view by a gaudy bandanna handkerchief—to the soles of her moccasin-clad feet she was bizarre, unusual. Her raven-black curls framing a face so entrancing that one could only wonder at the beauty of it. It was small, regular, perfectly formed, as was her body, which was as lithe as a boy's.

The suns of California had tanned her skin a dark, olive-bronze. In colorful contrast were her lips, as red as pomegranates. But what held one longest were her eyes,—large, dark, lustrous and filled with undimmed fire.

Don Fernando stiffened as he caught sight of

her. The señora and Alvarez, following his eyes, saw her a moment later. The attorney adjusted his glasses rather hurriedly after his first look at the girl.

"A beauty, if ever there was one," he admitted. "Peon or not, she is a flower."

"And accordingly—dangerous," Guiterrez declared. "And those clothes—the girl seems to prefer them to better garments. To my knowledge, she is continually receiving presents of one sort or another. Every vaquero on the place has made eyes at her; but she will have none of them. And as for independence, humph! She is stealing away right now for the afternoon. She knows that Ruiz is not here to forbid it."

As they watched her, Suzanna rode out of sight, blissfully unconscious that she was the subject of conversation of the trio seated upon the veranda. In her hands she held a crude fishing rod. Using it as a gad, she urged her burro toward the distant hills where the placid San Carmelo River wound along between moss covered banks. She hummed a song as she thumped the burro,—a bit of an endless sentimental strain:

"Te amo, si, te amo de veras;
No puedo mas ocultarlo;
Para que mi bien callarlo
Si conociendolo estas."

Allowing for the loss of rhythm and idiom which translation imposes, Suzanna's song said:

"I love you, yes, I love you truly;
No longer can I hold my tongue,
That I may well conceal my passion,
For you already guess my love."

It is doubtful, though, if the song conjured in her brain any picture of dashing *caballero* upon his knees before her repeating those identical words. Suzanna's dominating thought, at present, being to put as much distance between herself and the *Caserio de Gutierrez* as she possibly could, and during the shortest space of time, for intuitively, and by past performances, too, Suzanna sensed work should her father catch sight of her. That the next half-hour would find him back at the hacienda she did not doubt.

There was work in plenty to be done this afternoon; but grinding grain, carrying water, cooking and baking had long since palled on her. Let the old crones, who had a heart for such things, bestir themselves! On account of her dictatorial airs they called her a no-good, anyway. It mattered but little to the girl. The men about the rancho paid her homage of an ardor only limited by her own pleasure, and Suzanna, for all her lack of education and culture, had long since digested the fact that it was the men who mattered.

Suzanna had often stolen away for an afternoon along the San Carmelo, and once she was within the protecting hills which bordered the stream, she allowed her burro to make his own pace. It was an afternoon well suited for day dreaming, and she had an endless number of air-castles to build.

A week gone she had met a stranger in these very hills,—a knightly man, for all that he had proven overly bold. Suzanna had scorned him, but the thought that she might meet him again intruded on her revery more than once as she rode along.

Pico, her burro, was in perfect accord with the lazy day, and he dragged himself and his burden over the hot trail. Eventually, however, he brought Suzanna to the river's edge, where he stood lackadaisically switching his tail. Suzanna prodded him, but he refused to move. With darkening eyes, she brought her pole into play. Pico only flicked an indifferent ear in answer.

Where the burro had stopped, it was intolerably hot. Across the river was a cool, shady, moss-covered bank, agreeable to the eye and inviting to the body. Remained but to ford the stream to attain it. The water was delightfully cool and the fording shallow; but Pico had no liking for it.

The girl's temper rose as she sought to drive the stubborn beast across. *"Madre de Dios, Pico,"* she stormed, "I'll put this rod into your vitals if you don't make haste."

Pico silently dared her to do her worst. Suzanna found his hide an excellent barrier against her efforts. Ten minutes must have elapsed as the struggle went on. Suddenly the roar of a gun in the burro's immediate rear broke the stillness of the river bottom. Pico bounded for the opposite bank in punishing leaps, Suzanna clinging to him as best she could.

A laugh, and the sound of someone fording the stream, reached her as she slipped from the burro's back. With pounding heart and eyes wide with fear she turned to protect herself. Before her, hat in hand as he bowed to the ground, stood the stranger whom she had met before, Benito Pérez!

"*Buenas tardes, querida mia,*" he murmured unctiously. "You are a ravishing surprise for so hot a day."

CHAPTER V

"DOES THE NAME MATTER?"

SUZANNA's eyes flashed as she saw who addressed her, even though she did not by any chance suspect him to be the outlaw Pérez. As has been said, the man had a way with him which caught the fancy. Suzanna had not escaped it, neither had she failed to recognize the unbroken spirit of him. She had trimmed her sails accordingly, for, to a certainty, the man was little likely to pay heed once he was out of hand.

Seeing in him but an over-ripe *caballero*, Suzanna felt no great fear at his discovery of her so far from the *caserío*. The manner of his approach and his terms of endearment deserved a rebuke however, and she was not slow in acquainting him with as much.

" *'Querida mia?'* " she echoed sarcastically. "Since when? Do you lie in hiding like a wolf, ready to pounce upon me the minute I stir from the *caserío?* Answer me!" she snapped. "You are more presumptuous than ever."

Pérez gazed at her good-naturedly, if impudently, delighting in her show of temper.

“Come little one,” he said chidingly, “why scold me for being presumptuous when it is the very quality a woman most admires in a man? You would do well not to turn those flashing eyes on me, for they but match your lips, and steal away my senses.”

“Pretty words,” Suzanna answered with fine contempt. “I shall know how you found me here.”

“That’s easily told,” Pérez grinned; “from the top of that brown hill in back of us. I had but stopped in the shade of those live-oaks to breathe my horse when I caught sight of you. But those clothes,—they are no fit garb for one of your surpassing beauty.”

“*Madre de Dios!*” Suzanna exclaimed. “And now you are to tell me what I shall wear, eh?” Stepping close to Pérez, she snapped her fingers within an inch of his face. “Suppose you go back to your hill and your own business,” she cried. “I have busybodies enough watching me already.”

“Oh, you are adorable when you frown,” Pérez whispered. “Come, see what I have here for you, —a marvelous silk, a true mogador! I—ah—acquired it but to-day. Can you resist it, Suzanna?"

Suzanna's frown disappeared as she regarded the silk held so temptingly in the bandit's hands. She dropped her head and glanced up coquettishly at Pérez. The man's eyes held hers as a smile parted her lips.

"It's yours, *niña mia,*" he said softly. "I asked the gentleman from whom I secured it for something of surpassing beauty because it was for one I held surpassingly fair. The silk is beautiful, but not more so than you."

Suzanna reached out her hands and ran her fingers over the gay mogador. As she did, Pérez tossed the piece of goods into her arms and caught her around the waist.

"Come," he murmured passionately, "is there no pay for poor me?"

Suzanna sunk her nails into his flesh as he held his mouth so provokingly close to hers. "So, that's the way you give, eh?" she screamed. "Before the gift is cold you are asking for pay!"

"Truly it is a coarse word, *niña mia,*" Pérez said with a great show of penitence. "Let's call it reward; and since you withhold it, poor me must collect for himself."

Suzanna struggled and clawed, but the robber chief crushed her in his arms and planted a kiss upon her lips.

"Hast no one told you that stolen fruit is sweetest?" he asked boldly.

"Yes; but even the sweetest fruit turns sour!" Suzanna cried menacingly. "Do you feel that gun boring into your thick skin, señor?" The fact that Pérez' smile froze upon his lips was proof enough that he did. "It is your own pistol," she warned. "You unhand me or we'll see how well it shoots!"

He continued to hold her for a second, daring her to fire, and then, with courtly air he released her. "You make me love you, little one," he murmured, as he stepped back. "I'll treasure those scratches you have put upon my face."

"You make great haste with your love, don't you?" Suzanna said bitingly. "You must have great success with it."

"No measure but what I'd trade for a smile from you."

"The words fly too easily to your lips," Suzanna taunted him. "I've not even the name of you yet."

"And does the name matter?" Pérez asked seriously. "Is it not enough that you see I am no belted friar? I am a free-man—the while, at least—is not that enough for you, pretty one?"

"Well you know that it is not," Suzanna answered coldly. "And now that I see it is by design and not accident that you withhold it, I am doubly warned. When free-man bows his head to peon girl the reason is not far to seek. Take your precious silk, and begone."

Pérez shook his head as she held out his gift.

"Very well," Suzana exclaimed angrily. "Since you will have it no other way, take it from the ground!" And she tossed the goods at his feet.

"There are other pieces, *querida*, even finer than that one, which I shall bring to you," he said evenly. "Another time I shall please you better."

Pérez had dropped his boasting tone, and as he turned to his horse and mounted, Suzanna sighed uneasily. This man understood the art of love! She called to him as he reached the middle of the stream. Pérez wheeled his horse at sound of her voice.

"Your pistol, señor," Suzanna cried. With a muscular toss she hurled it through the air to him.

Pérez caught it deftly, and bowing, rode off without backward glance.

The man had his audience, as he half-suspected. Suzanna had not been prepared for his manner of leave-taking, and her eyes followed him as he rode away. Even when he was well across the stream, she believed that he would turn back, for a word at least. In this she was disappointed, for Pérez surmised her thought, and he was well enough versed in the ways of women to know that the unusual always succeeds with them.

Suzanna drew a deep breath as he passed out of sight. "*Madre de Dios,*" she murmured, "There goes a real *caballero!*"

Suzanna stood where she was for a spell, contemplating the fact that life along the San Carmelo River was vastly more interesting than it was at the *Rancho de Gutierrez.* The man had taken her breath away, a sensation hard work had never produced.

As the minutes passed, and she realized that the stranger was not coming back, she fell to her knees, and picking up the mogador, brushed away the sand which clung to it. And then, with a purely feminine gesture, she held it up to her waist to get the effect of it.

"Bless the saints," she whispered to herself, "there cannot be anything more beautiful. And yet, he talks of even finer things. Truly, the man who selected this was no fool. He must have looked at many before he made his choice."

CHAPTER VI

THE SURPRISING HISTORY OF A PIECE OF SILK

Suzanna's thoughts were far from fishing as she stretched her length upon the moss-covered bank beside the sluggish San Carmelo. As she lay there, day-dreaming, a crackling of brush behind her caused her to sit up in some agitation. Her first thought was that Pérez was returning. Quickly hiding the silk, she sat stiffly and waited. Imagine her surprise, then, when a six months' old cinnamon cub broke from cover almost at her feet.

The bear was not less frightened than she. Turning tail, he dashed back into the manzanita which bordered the river.

Suzanna's fear soon left her, and she became possessed of a mad desire to own that little cub. A large field of wheat lay beyond the narrow strip of underbrush, and she knew if she could drive the cub into it, that he would have little chance of getting away. Seizing Pico's lead rope, and fashioning it into a crude lariat, she dashed after the fleeing bear.

The cub made slower progress through the chaparral than did the girl. The noise of her coming, and her cries of pain as briars and thorns tore her skin, cost the bear his wits, and abandoning his native caution he bounded into the wheat field. The grain had been harvested some weeks ago, and the new shoots were only up some foot and a half.

Suzanna caught sight of the bear as soon as she was out of the brush, and with a wild halloo she set after him.

Thanks to her masculine attire, she soon managed to draw up on the cub. Judging herself close enough to slip the noose over his head, she sailed it through the air. The treacherous ground upset her, and she sprawled her length. The force with which she landed rung a grunt from her lips.

The sound was a new one to the cub's ears, and his curiosity not to be denied, he turned, impudently, and surveyed her. When Suzanna sat up the bear was still there, resting on his haunches.

The girl grinned at him as she rubbed her tortured body. "So, my fine fellow," she cried, "you sit and laugh at me, eh? You wait!"

Cautiously regaining her rope and coiling it, she sprang toward him, but the bear was not caught unaware. With a bound, he was off for the other end of the field. The King's Highway passed there, and the cub, hesitating to cross where there was no cover at all, circled back toward a huge straw stack fairly in line with the girl.

A game of tag began as they dashed round and round the stack. Suzanna's dog had joined the pair and the chase. Hearing a noise behind her, the girl felt that the bear had started to chase her, and without stopping to reason, ran for an old cypress tree, which stood beside the road, and took refuge in it.

The cub, however, had tired of the game some minutes before and had taken refuge in the same tree. At the moment that Suzanna was scrambling up, the cub was perched on a limb above her calmly surveying the scene.

Suzanna, having reached the first limb, backed out on it a few feet and then came to a sudden halt. Something was pressing against her back! Exactly what it was, she couldn't have told, but she knew it was alive! Casting a backward glance across her shoulder, she saw the bear. With a scream, she began moving out upon the limb. For now, that she was within a hair's breadth of it, *she* became the quarry, and not the cub. Roping a bear was one thing; capturing it with bare hands while astride the limb of a tree, fifteen feet above the ground, was something else again. Suzanna decided to continue retreating—and did—onto another limb on the other side of the tree. The cub, sensing Suzanna's waning interest, became playfully inclined, and started in pursuit. Suzanna slid backward toward the lower end of the limb. The cub crept toward her. Not realizing its intentions, the girl began shouting for help. She was in no particular danger, a moment's thought would have assured her of that, but she had become panic-stricken, and her cries carried conviction.

Ramon, riding at the head of his wagon-train, stood in his stirrups as he caught the faint sound of someone calling for help. The boy cast an anxious look ahead of him, and then turned to his peons to see if they betrayed any sign of having heard that strange call. The poor devils had crawled back to the wagon soon after Pérez and his band had disappeared, asking for the punishment they so richly deserved. Ramon had left their punishment to Ruiz, knowing that he would exact many extra hours in the fields from them for their cowardice.

The boy saw that they were on edge now, and with a call to his *sobrestante*, he dashed away toward the low ridge that topped the wide draw in which the wagon moved. On the crest, he stopped for an instant to better locate the source of those cries. He was near enough the tree to which Suzanna and the bear had retreated to be able to see a form dangling from a lower limb. Giving his horse the spurs, he sped toward the old cypress.

"Hold there!" he called to what he believed to be a full-grown boy: "Let go when I give the word. Now!"

Suzanna's face had been turned upward as she clung to the limb, and due to her excitement she had not recognized Ramon's voice. He was equally ignorant of whom he rescued. And so, when he caught her and they looked into each other's eyes, astonishment gripped both of them.

"Holy Mother," Suzanna gasped. "You?"

"None other, *marimacho*," Ramon answered vexedly. "What is it you do here?"

"Hast eyes, petulant one?" Suzanna scolded.

The boy's teeth flashed in a wide grin as he caught sight of the cub. "Oh, ho!" he chuckled the while he nodded his head mockingly. "You best be careful whose trees you climb. Were you trying to capture him?"

"Humph! I was trying to get *away* from him."

Ramon's laughter grew as she told him of the incident.

"Your father and his men can take care of the cub. I'll carry you back to Pico, and see you safely to the hacienda. The country is too unsettled these days for you to be wandering off in this manner. And how, by the way, do you make of this a holiday?"

"Are you cross with me, my Ramon?" Suzanna asked naïvely.

"Have I ever been, *camarada?*"

Suzanna pinched his cheek playfully and ended by giving it an affectionate pat. "My father will scold when he hears that I have been away since noon." She stopped speaking until her eyes held the boy's. "He does not scold—much—when you tell him that your father is not displeased."

"*Si,* I understand," Ramon nodded. "I shall intercede for you, *once more!*"

He reached for her playfully, and Suzanna in trying to dodge away from his arms dropped the piece of silk which had been hidden in her blouse. Ramon's hand shot out and captured it before it reached the ground. The boy instantly recognized the mogador. "How do you come by this?" he demanded sharply.

"Art jealous?" Suzanna asked saucily. "And surprised, my Ramon? Am I so plain that you marvel to find others making presents to me?"

The boy had gripped her wrists savagely. The pressure of his fingers, as well as the grim set of his jaw, sobered the girl. Open-mouthed she stared at him.

"Present?" Ramon whipped out angrily. "I selected that piece of silk for you myself,—this very day aboard a smuggling ship from Boston, now anchored in Monterey Bay!"

"*You* selected it?" Suzanna gasped, unable to understand the boy's words. "You say that you selected it for me," she exclaimed, "and yet I have it here,—the gift of one who is a stranger to you. If you selected it how came it out of your possession?"

"It was taken from me not an hour since," cried

Ramon, his anger unabated. "We were attacked by the bandit, Benito Pérez, as we came to *El Paso del Viento.*"

"Benito Pérez!" Suzanna let the man's name tremble upon her tongue.

"Holy Mother of God!" she muttered chokingly as she crossed herself. "I've been kissed by the most famous robber in California!"

CHAPTER VII

CHIQUITA DE SOLA

ALTHOUGH Don Fernando had not communicated his misgivings to his friend, Diego de Sola, that gentleman was most miserable on his own account; life in Mexico City having proved anything but what he had anticipated. His interests were largely centered in his hacienda in California, and however blue the day, he drew solace from the fact that he would soon be returning to that land of sunshine, where, God be praised, his daughter would soon be safely wed.

Disquieting news at this time would have been too much, for Don Diego's cup of misery was already overflowing, his daughter's education proving a greater task than his gray hairs could manage. He paced his tastefully appointed study on this particular night, agitation and worry plainly written upon his handsome face.

He paused as someone knocked for admission. In reply to his command to enter, the door opened

to admit a middle-aged woman. Quietly closing
the door behind her, she hesitated, in evident embarrassment, before speaking.

Don Diego sensed her confusion. "No need to
ask," he exclaimed. "You bring bad news."

The woman bowed her head unhappily. "I regret that it is so," she answered. "Señora Carrera
positively refuses to permit Chiquita to return to
her studies."

Señor de Sola flung himself into a chair at this
news, holding his tongue by a supreme effort. At
sight of his anger, the woman hastened to add:

"I have pleaded—threatened almost—but she
will not relent. She says the girl has too often
violated the rules of the school to deserve another
chance. She even refers to her as a girl without
—the—er—sense of right or wrong. "I——"

"Precisely what is my daughter accused of doing?" Don Diego demanded with asperity.

Instead of answering, the woman resorted to
tears. "I—I—do not want to say," she managed
to stammer at last.

"But you shall!" Chiquita's father exclaimed.
"I command you to tell me! You are her *duenna;*
you have been closer to her than I have; I em-

ployed you to keep her reputation consistent with the position she and I occupy. If the girl has done wrong, then you are partly to blame. You should have restrained her,—kept me informed. Now she is sent home in disgrace; and yet you hesitate to tell me what the girl has done?"

De Sola's angry words but increased the misery of the poor woman before him. "I have tried to protect her," she said between sobs. "I have aided her in every way; but she has taken advantage of me."

"But what has she done?" the irate father thundered as he got to his feet.

"She has been escaping from school and meeting young men clandestinely."

"What?" Don Diego's usually calm brown eyes grew almost black as this startling news greeted his ears. White-lipped, he approached the *duenna.* "Is this true?" he cried excitedly. "Do you mean to tell me that my daughter has so far forgotten herself and her breeding as to be guilty of such baseness?"

"Señora Carrera insists that it is. She went so far as to say that her school would be ruined if fathers and mothers learned that one of her pupils had committed such misdeeds. That is why she even refuses to think of taking her back."

"Where have your eyes been?" Don Diego demanded. "Have you been blind that you did not see or suspect as much? I trusted you with the honor of my family,—and now I am forced to bow my head in shame. Poor witless wretch, I owe you a debt, indeed. Pack your things and be gone!"

"It were easy to blame me," the *duenna* answered with a show of spirit. "Had your own child as much consideration for your good name as I have had there would be no talk of shame. My back has never been turned before she was up to mischief. I am glad to go. Never has a woman been tried as I have been."

Don Diego made no attempt to answer her, and starting for the door, the woman stopped as she passed a window overlooking the moon-lit garden.

"See!" she exclaimed, pointing toward the patio. "There is added proof if you want it! The girl has not been in the house ten minutes, but already she finds time for further misconduct."

De Sola pointed to the door. "Go!" he ordered sternly, but no sooner had the woman quitted the

room than he leaped to the window and raked the
garden with his eyes.

It was a beautiful evening,—a night made for
love and lovers. From above shone the moon in all
its full resplendence; scintillating stars wreath-like
around it. Iridescent moon-beams cast shimmer-
ing shadows on the rose-strewn, trellised garden.
As the don's eyes became accustomed to the light,
he made out two figures in the shadow of the patio
wall; one a man—a stranger; the other a girl—his
daughter.

Uttering an angry exclamation, he turned from
the window and, pausing only to buckle on his
sword, he rushed downstairs and into the garden.

Chiquita lay in the man's arms, unaware of ap-
proaching disaster. She was a radiantly beautiful
girl, or rather woman, for there was little of the
shy, unsophisticated girl, which she had been when
she first came to Mexico City, left in her.

Her sultry beauty seemed to intoxicate the stranger. Her lips, rich, full, had tasted his kisses and
she lay back now, daring him on with her smoky
eyes. The stranger accepted her challenge, and
pressed her to him again and again.

"Ah, Pancho," she murmured dreamily, "thou art a wonderful lover."

"And thou art a still more wonderful sweetheart," the man breathed softly into her ear. "Thine eyes are as the most precious stones, thy hair as sheer as finest silk, thy brow fairer than any gentle sun or whispering wind ever kissed; thy lips are more perfect than a cupid's bow, sweeter than honey, softer than eiderdown, more colorful than a pomegranate. Thou art the personification of Venus and all her beautiful sisters combined. Thou——"

"Enough, *enamorato mio*," Chiquita interrupted with a warm little laugh. "Thou art as good at piercing my poor heart and brain with thy flattery as thou art at piercing the heart of a maddened bull with thy sword. But what thy lips fail to say, thy eyes revealeth. Thou art thinking that I——"

Chiquita broke off with startling suddenness, as she looked up and saw her father striding angrily toward her. The man saw him, too, and immediately released her.

"Your father!" he murmured hastily, lifting a derisive hand in the direction of Don Diego. "I'll stand before an angry bull, but a maddened father, —never!"

Chiquita was too badly flustered to heed his wit. Dumbly, she saw him vault easily to the top of the wall which enclosed the garden. Safe, he paused bravely enough and plucked a rose, pressed it to his lips and tossed it toward her.

Don Diego reached for him with his sword as the stranger disappeared in the darkness on the other side of the wall, his insolent laugh floating back to the father's ears. But even though Don Diego caught the rose which the stranger had thrown Chiquita, he failed to recognize the fleeing lover.

Don Diego crushed the flower between his fingers and throwing it to the earth, ground it into the dirt with his heel. Silently then, for an interval, they took stock of each other; the proud, self-centered girl's lips curling with contempt for the indulgent parent who had treated her so cavalierly; the father's face suffused with shame that his own flesh and blood had tarnished the honour of his house.

"What manner of woman are you?" he asked when he could trust his voice. "Have you forgotten every teaching? It is not enough that you are bundled home from school, but ten minutes after you arrive you must prove to me with my own eyes that Señora Carrera did not libel you!"

"I am old enough for love," Chiquita answered flatly.

"Love?" her father cried incredulously. "You shame the word. Do you call it love, to deliver yourself to the embraces of one who comes and goes by way of the garden wall? Have I the man's acquaintance? Does he come with honorable intentions? You need not answer! This man—I had no look at his face, but by the cut of his clothes some blustering *torero*—shall answer to me, no matter what his station."

"But first, you shall find him," the girl declared impudently. "Think you, my father, that I am satisfied to spend my days answering to the whims of crusty teacher or wrinkled *duenna*? I did not come to Mexico City to take Holy Orders!"

"Stop!" Don Diego fumed. "You came here to learn the airs and graces befitting one of your high estate. I had no mind for leaving California. It was to please you that we came here. You wanted advantages that were not to be had at home. And you repay me with this! Have you forgotten that you are already betrothed? What would Ramon and his family think if they knew of your conduct?"

"Small difference it would make to me," Chiquita answered with a toss of her head. "If I am betrothed to Ramon it is because it pleased you, not me."

"God pity me that I should live to hear such words from your lips," her father cried. "There is not a girl in the New World but what would be honored with Ramon Gutierrez for husband. He is a worthy son. His father tells me that Ramon waits with impatience for your return. This night shall a letter be dispatched to Don Fernando telling him that we leave immediately."

Chiquita heard this ultimatum with ill-concealed regret. Angry tears filled her eyes. Her father, mis-reading her emotion, made as though to place his hand upon her shoulder.

"Chiquita, my child," he said sadly, "you are all your father has; why do you act in this manner? Come to my arms and promise me that you will——"

But the girl turned from him, and without a word, hurried up the path toward the house.

Once in her room, Chiquita resorted to tears.

She told herself that she preferred death to going back to California.

"I hate it," she sobbed. "There's no place to go; nothing to do; no crowds, no life; no music,—I'll die of loneliness."

And in her madness she dropped to her knees and begged her patron saint to put some obstacle in her father's path that would forever keep him from returning to California and its barren hills.

CHAPTER VIII

THE BLOOD STRAIN

Señor Alvarez, the lawyer, returned to the *Hacienda de Gutierrez* ten days after his conference with Ramon's father. Miguel, his son, had remained at the hacienda during this time, and it was the lawyer's intention to return this day to Monterey with the boy, his vacation having ended.

Even his adoring father must have noted the change in Miguel. The boy was more robust and in spirit grown actually mischievous. He had pestered Don Fernando's vaqueros so persistently that, in self-defense, they had taught him how to throw a rope and sit upon a horse.

Miguel's efforts to reward his teachers had been tireless, but not altogether successful. Suzanna had laughed openly at his awkwardness. In fact, the truculence and impudence of this peon girl was the one fly in an otherwise perfect vacation for the boy. He resented the airs she gave herself, and this was not helped any by seeing that Don Fernando and his family humored her and by their graciousness gave her courage for fresh indignities.

Miguel, as wise in his way as his father was, had said nothing, but he had sought for a means by which he could humble the girl. This very last day of his sojourn at the rancho seemed to hold a promise of success for him.

Suzanna's proudest possession—with the possible exception of the bear which her father had captured for her—was a small, thoroughbred fighting gamecock, Timoteo, by name.

Timoteo had vanquished all local foes, and Suzanna paid him the homage due a champion. The hacienda was the extent of her world, and she refused to believe that beyond its borders there might be a bird able to take away Timoteo's crown. Human beings are prone to grow extravagant in their speech regarding things which they consider certainties. It was so with Suzanna. If one wanted to draw her wrath, he had but to question Timoteo's prowess. Miguel had, inadvertently, and then, seeing the effect it produced, had resorted to it daily as fair reward for the indignities the girl offered him.

Miguel's knowledge of gamecocks was most limited, but happily Suzanna was blind to this fact. The boy pretended to a wide experience with the fighting birds, and from the heights to which this knowledge raised him in Suzanna's eyes he had made many telling, and very derisive, remarks about her champion.

The girl's misery well repaid the boy. But lacking that delicate sense which warns against a too heavy hand, Miguel overstepped himself, and Suzanna, daring anything in her anger, scoffingly invited him to produce a fighter which could defeat her precious Timoteo. The defy having been hurled in the presence of the vaqueros whom the boy had tried to impress, left Miguel but one answer, for all that it was hardly the custom for his class to resort to the fighting pit with a peon.

Early on the morning of this very day, Miguel had set out to find Timoteo's conqueror. He had given himself so much knowledge that he dared not ask advice, at this late date, of those who really knew. Monterey was too far away, so the boy had turned to the south where a large force of Mexican peons were constructing a crude bridge across the Rio Salinas. From them he hoped to purchase a bird that would tear Suzanna's presumptuous contender to ribbons.

Timoteo was a small, blue-black, vicious-eyed gamecock. Miguel came back from his quest bearing a bird three times the size of Suzanna's pet. The peon, from whom the boy had purchased him, had assured Miguel that the rooster had no peer with the steel spurs. The man, seeing that he dealt with a child, had pointed to the bird's size as further proof of his ability, and Miguel, not knowing that the very size of the rooster proclaimed him a cross-breed, had paid his money, and headed for the north well satisfied with himself.

Moving with caution, he had smuggled the bird into his room to await the coming bout. No word of it reached the members of Don Fernando's household or Miguel's father; but the news spread quickly among those employed on the hacienda.

The bout was scheduled to take place at sundown. Miguel waited until the bell announced the evening meal, and then, his bird in a bag, he stole out of the casa and made for the corral in back of the peons' quarters. He found the audience already assembled, with Suzanna standing impatiently in the center of the ring, holding Timoteo in the crook of her arm.

The gamecock struggled and uttered his battle-cry the instant that Miguel brought forth his rooster. Suzanna laughed as she saw the size of Miguel's contender. The pit-wise onlookers grinned also. The boy interpreted this greeting correctly, and his assurance left him as he saw that his rooster made no attempt to answer Timoteo's cry. With a savage pinch he rang a protesting squawk from the bird.

"Ha, ha!" Suzanna cried. "That bird is neither fit for pot or pit. Wait, Timoteo," she cooed to her pet, "we shall laugh soon enough."

"We shall see," Miguel retorted acidly. "Make your precious bird ready.

The steel spurs were quickly attached, and with a movement of the referee's hand Miguel and Suzanna tossed their fowls into the ring.

As though shot out of a gun, Timoteo leaped for the big rooster, ripping him with his spurs. Miguel's bird lost all interest immediately. With a frightened cry he sailed into the air and over the heads of the watchers, Timoteo after him. The audience shrieked. Suzanna uttered a wild cry

and pursued the fowls. Miguel, thoroughly crest-
fallen, followed her.

It had been no fight at all, and now, all but the
boy, held their sides as the farce proceeded. The
rooster and the gamecock darted round and round
the corral fence and in and out beneath the farm
implements and wagons parked beside it.

"Turn them back!" Suzanna cried to Miguel as
the fowls headed in his direction, and Miguel, in a
white rage at the rooster who had let him in for this
ridicule, leaped forward, but he fell short of turning them. The open kitchen door lay beyond, and
risking all on a wild dash, the rooster lined straight
for it.

A cry of dismay rose from the crowd at this.
This cock fight had been held without the sanction
of Don Fernando, a trivial enough matter, but the
peons knew that the evening meal was still in progress within the casa, and that the dining room lay
just beyond the kitchen. Should Timoteo chase
the fleeing rooster into that holy of holies,—*cui-
dado!*—trouble would follow.

Miguel added his groans to the peons' cries when
he got up from the dust. If the calamity, which the

servants feared, came to pass, he was in for a very embarrassing hour.

Suzanna's nimble brain grasped the situation, too, but unlike the others, she rushed after her pet. She called to Timoeto as she ran, but Timoteo was a bird of one purpose at present. Another second, and Miguel's rooster darted into the kitchen; in his immediate rear, the rushing gamecock.

The crowd did not wait for the verdict, but slunk away, intent on disavowing any connection with the affair. Miguel saw Suzanna enter the kitchen, and with a sort of dying hope that the inevitable might still be averted, he dashed after her. His heart failed him as he gained the door and saw that the way to the dining room was unbarred.

No sound of the tumult outside had penetrated the cool, darkened room in which Don Fernando's family and Señor Alvarez sat. Ramon's father sat at one end of the long board experiencing the comfortable feeling of a man whose stomach is well-filled and whose mind is at peace with the world. The house-servants had just removed the dishes, and with hand-rolled cigars and a rare vintage before him, Don Fernando surveyed his friend, Alvarez, and his son, Ramon, with keen pleasure.

Ramon's father and the lawyer had held a consultation that afternoon, and it had been planned that at this very time the boy should hear the ultimatum in regard to Suzanna.

It was a propitious moment. The meal had passed with rare pleasure, and Don Fernando congratulated himself on choosing this time for broaching the subject. He shot a keen glance in the direction of his son, and was further pleased to note that Ramon was in excellent spirits. The aged don showed his astuteness by addressing himself to Alvarez rather than to the boy.

"How do things fare in Monterey?" he asked quite casually.

The lawyer had awaited this question, and he promptly voiced his rehearsed answer.

"From bad to worse," he replied with a show of feeling. "The Mission property is about destroyed. Some of the small ranchers are hiring the Indians at a daily wage. If this thing is not put down, we will be hard-pressed to gather our crops. We cannot exist without peon labor. This talk of educating them is heresy. Once we start that, they will be out of hand completely."

"Well, I wonder," Don Fernando replied, seeming to weigh his answer.

"What? Have you turned Republican, too?"

"Hardly! But I have begun to question some of our institutions."

Ramon heard his father's words in amazement. This was an unbending which he had never dreamed possible. Don Fernando read his son's thoughts, and made his cast.

"What I am about to say will come as a great surprise, I know," the master of the hacienda continued. "I have gone so far as to formulate certain plans regarding the educating of one of my peons. But last evening did I receive confirmation of them."

"Ruiz?" the lawyer asked interestedly.

"No," Don Fernando replied deliberately, and with a shaking of his head,— "his daughter, Suzanna."

"What?" Ramon asked. "Have you spoken to her? She has——"

"Ramon!" Doña Luz remonstrated. "Allow your father to finish."

Señor Gutierrez bowed, and went on:

"Suzanna is an unusual girl. A beautiful woman, I might add. She seems to possess intelligence beyond the scope of the average peon. Enough so, that she manages to unload her work upon the shoulders of others. Her lack of industry is the girl's worst fault.

"But you know," continuing to address himself to Alvarez, "that my wife and I have long felt a peculiar attachment for her. Her father has been a loyal servant. That, as well as my interest in the girl herself has led me to make this move."

"It is a worthy effort, although it may prove a foolhardy one," Doña Luz declared uneasily.

"Surely it is a wonderful chance for the girl," Alvarez cried heartily. "Why there is not one peon in ten thousand who can write his own name. The girl is beautiful; but, in all kindness, one must admit that she is without culture of any sort."

"If there is any possibility of her acquiring it," Don Fernando answered, "she will do so at San Luis Bautista."

"San Luis Bautista?" Ramon echoed incredulously.

"Yes. I received word last evening from Padre Altado saying he would receive her."

"Why, San Luis Bautista is many leagues away,"

the boy exclaimed. "She will be gone from the hacienda for a matter of months. She is intensely happy here. Have you given any thought to the fact that she is going to be miserable and lonesome in San Luis Bautista?"

"It is a means to an end, my boy. For it, she must be willing to suffer."

A sadness which he could not explain had settled upon the boy's heart. For the first time his eyes were open to the fact that Suzanna was very, very dear to him. In kaleidoscopic procession, his lifetime association with her passed across his mental mirror. In his boy and man world there had been no one to approach her in comradeship. He had grown to take her for granted. The sudden announcement that she was to be taken away from him for a period that might well be as long as two years, filled him with consternation. The loss of impudent, tomboyish Suzanna assumed the proportions of a calamity. And although pressed as he was for time, he asked himself why this should be so.

The lingering caress of her fingers upon his cheek, the sweet fragrance of her breath, memories of her unafraid eyes and the thrill which had suffused his body that very morning when he, in lifting her from her saddle, had held her close for a brief second, came back to smite him. The passive male in him disappeared in a twinkling as such pictures continued to flash in his brain. Long dormant primordial instincts took possession of him. Boyhood passed, and manhood gripped him. The sex impulse was in it, and the thirst to protect his own.

Suzanna was his mate, his woman. He saw it, oh, so clearly, now. What mattered it that she was a peon? This talk of blood strains had no place in California. Before God, the two of them stood together,—a man and a woman! The thought brought him to his feet.

His mother caught his agitation and she pressed her hands together nervously as he raised his voice.

"Have you told Suzanna that she goes so far as San Luis Bautista?" Ramon demanded.

Don Fernando winced at the thought that he should be expected to consult with his servants about a matter which pointed to their own welfare.

"Certainly not," he cried. "I am the master of this hacienda! Do you, my son, suggest that *I* confer with one of my peons before I raise my hand to act?"

"Perhaps 'twere well you did, my father," Ramon answered stoutly. "It is nothing short of cruelty to take a girl, who has never been beyond the boundaries of this rancho, to a strange place, among strange faces, and where at best she will receive scant respect from those about her."

The boy's voice rang out so intensely that those at the table were not aware of Suzanna who had crept in from the kitchen in search of Timoteo and his quarry. Miguel's rooster had taken refuge in a great wicker basket beside the door. Timoteo, missing him completely, was searching vainly beneath the table for him.

Suzanna had not caught the mention of her name, but she sensed immediately the strife between father and son. The distraught face of Doña Luz and the excited eyes of the attorney filled her with alarm. For all her trepidation, Suzanna knew that if Don Fernando caught her intruding at this unfortunate moment that no light punishment would be visited on her. So, consigning Timoteo to the tender mercies of the saints, she turned cautiously toward the kitchen. She had taken but one tiny step when the wrathful don's voice boomed in her ears. With every muscle quivering nervously, Suzanna cowered where she stood.

Don Fernando had not seen her. His attention was riveted solely upon his son.

"Your saintly mother and I know what is best for Suzanna!" he thundered wrathfully.

Suzanna recoiled at sound of her name. Her hand went to her mouth as she realized that she was the cause of this scene.

"I thought you would be pleased at what I intend," Don Fernando exclaimed. "You have grown up together; I know your feeling for the girl, and I am only sorry that your present interest in her is misplaced. You should know that neither your mother nor I would do aught to hurt her. Men call me stern, but, praise God, not unjust. Remember this, my boy,—you are the descendant of kings! Suzanne is a peon. It is part of your legacy that you guide the weaker. You cannot temper wisdom with sentiment. Suzanna goes south by next train to San Luis Bautista!"

In fitting answer to this outburst came a wild cry. Timoteo had caught sight of a stuffed eagle reposing upon a stand in a corner of the room, and its life-like appearance must have fooled the game-cock into believing that here at last was the cowardly rooster.

Doña Luz gasped with astonishment as a feathered fury leaped from beneath the table and landed upon the eagle's back. Alvarez was on his feet, his chair tipping over in back of him as he struggled to get free of it.

Ramon grinned as he recognized Timoteo. Don Fernando wheeled upon seeing his son smile, and found himself looking into Suzanna's wet eyes.

The worthy man's eyes snapped as he beheld the girl. Doña Luz gasped as she saw her husband's face grow red as he fought for speech.

"Let me speak to the girl," she begged.

For once Don Fernando was deaf to her entreaties. Suzanna's nervousness but added to her guilt in her master's eyes. He was convinced that she had stolen into the room to overhear what was being said.

Suzanna edged toward the door as Don Fernando glowered at her.

"Stop!" he cried. "Stand where you are until you have explained your presence in this room."

Dumbly, Suzanna bent her knee to him, and whispered "yes."

"What is the meaning of this intrusion?" the mighty owner of the *Rancho de Gutierrez* roared. "Have you been eavesdropping?"

Miguel had been drawn by the excitement and now stood in the doorway beside poor Suzanna. She saw him dimly through her tears as she choked back a sob and replied to her master.

"No, Don Fernando," she said brokenly. "I was only trying to prove to—to this young gentleman—that a mongrel cannot compete with a thoroughbred."

CHAPTER IX

A STRANGER IS MADE WELCOME

WHERE *El Camino Real* cut across a broad expanse of fertile valley land, a most striking figure rode. His pigtail proclaimed him a toreador by profession. Even seen at a distance, the man gave evidence of possessing unusual bodily strength. With becoming grace, he sat upon his horse, a beautiful, coal-black animal. He was slender, and his colorful clothes but added to the dare-devil air which the reckless tilt of his mouth prophesied.

The hilts of a pair of rapiers protruded from his saddle bags; behind him swung his guitar. Speed seemed to be a matter of no concern to him, for he repeatedly pulled his horse to a walk. The morning was still young, and the air keen with earthy smells.

The stranger cast a speculative eye at the fields which skirted the road. That the prospect pleased him was not to be doubted for he smiled from time to time and pursed his lips to whistle a bold lay.

And yet, for all his care-free manner, the man seemed out of key with these rural surroundings. Indeed, he had but recently quitted Mexico City where his prowess had won him some little fame.

He awakened from his dreaming and ceased whistling as he made a turn in the road and saw an elderly friar advancing in his direction. Halting his horse, he waited for the priest to come up to him.

The rotund friar nodded pleasantly, and the stranger, uncovering his head humbly, addressed the Franciscan. "Good morning, good padre," he murmured in tones both musical and flexible. "I trust your health is of the best."

The friar took good note of the man's costly raiment and the style of his hair. Priest he might be, but even so, he was a Spaniard, and not without a certain fondness for those of the bull-ring. "Thank you, my son," he answered with extreme good-will. "May the saints guard you; my health is most excellent. 'Tis passing long since I have seen one of your calling."

The stranger smiled at this directness.

"You live in a new country with little time for play," he expostulated. "I have almost convinced myself that it were well that I was done with it, too. Tell me, I pray, where lies the hacienda of Don Diego de Sola?"

"Just a short distance beyond," the friar answered. "In fact thou art gazing on the fields of Don Diego now. By continuing, within the hour you will come to the *caserio*. It lies to the left of the highway. Opposite, on your right, you will see the buildings of the *Rancho de Gutierrez*. You cannot lose your way. Without presuming, I might mention that you will not find Don Diego at home. He has been in Mexico City these many months."

"Yes, I know, kind father. He is returning shortly," the stranger replied. "Thank you for your good offices, and may the blessings of God and his saints be upon you."

The rider leaned from his saddle and dropped a coin into the padre's outstretched hand. With the holy man's blessing upon him, he spurred his horse and soon left the priest far behind.

Reaching the ridge of the hill pointed out to him by the friar, the man halted his horse and stood for a moment gazing out over the surrounding country—a broad expanse of beautiful land. For as far as his eyes could see, there was rolling country, dotted here and there with greenish-colored patches, but for the most part barren, except for wild grass and mesquite.

To his right were moderately high hills, sloping upward until their brownish tips kissed the sky; vast herds of cattle wandering sluggishly over them.

To his left, moving objects, a mile or so distant, caught his eye, and he inspected them carefully. Shortly, he made them out to be mounted men driving before them a herd of horses. They were converging upon a shallow draw beside the road from which a dust cloud rose already. Sending his horse into a hand-gallop, the stranger soon drew close enough to see what went forward.

A large corral had been constructed here beside the road, and to it Don Fernando's vaqueros now brought the unbroken horses which had roamed the range since the preceding fall. A smother of dust and the pungent smell of sweaty leather filled the air. Señor Gutierrez was in Monterey, so his retainers made a holiday of the horse-breaking. Whenever the dust lifted, their grinning faces could be seen ringed around the corral fence.

Young Ramon stood back some distance from the fence, busy with a string of figures. The stranger's eyes singled him out at once. Ramon, however, was not aware of him. The peons, though, cast many surreptitious glances at the imposing newcomer.

Ramon had taken his stand beside a hollow log, and what was the stranger's surprise to see a slender arm shoot out from within the log and toss a handful of dirt at him! Watching, the man saw Ramon start and look downward. The scene was repeated several times. Ramon glared with annoyance at the nearest man, but found nothing to convict him.

Additional vaqueros with still another string of horses swept down from the hills. Both Ramon and the man at the roadside followed them as they came on. Suddenly, several of the riders uttered a cry, and breaking into a wild gallop swung toward the corral. The watchers were not long in seeing the reason for this. The men had forced a young coyote from cover and they were after him now with the laudable purpose of roping him.

The peons sent up a cry of joy as they caught the spirit of the chase. Their noise but added to the poor animal's confusion, and losing his head the coyote dashed directly toward the corral.

A coyote will not take refuge in a hollow log or stump when possessed of his native cunning, but this was a young pup, and whatever cunning he was born to had left him. The log beside which Ramon had stood caught his eye, and with a bound he was at it, wriggling his way into its protecting embrace.

A scream broke from the other end of the log almost simultaneously. A second later a human being scrambled into view and dashed away in the direction of the *caserio*. The crowd howled its pleasure. Ramon shook his head as he recognized the fleeing figure. It was Suzanna!

"Esa chica es insoportable," the boy muttered to himself, and with truth it seemed that Suzanna had indeed become unmanageable as the day for her departure for San Luis Bautista drew near.

As much to hide his own chagrin as to turn the crowd's mind from the rapidly disappearing girl, Ramon sent his men to their places in preparation for the coming herd. For the time being, he was reconciled to having Suzanna sent to the Mission. She should not have ventured to the corral, and her embarrassment could not be greater than his.

With flashing eyes, and the bit of the devil in his teeth, he flung himself into the work at hand.

Dressed as he was, he seemed surprisingly thin and narrow about the hips. It is a way with boys raised in the saddle. He elected to tame a wild-eyed piebald cayuse, which had been saddled only after a bad twenty minutes. With a wave of his hand, he ordered his vaqueros to let go. A flying leap landed him squarely in the heavy saddle. For a second the battle was his; but the horse had only been stunned by the suddenness of his action. With an angry snort the animal leaped into the air and came down stiffly upon all fours. It is a back-breaking experience for the rider. Ramon clung on, and with his spurs straightened out the horse.

The spectators applauded vociferously as the boy sent the animal round and round the corral, meeting every trick the horse tried. Ramon was no mean rider and inside of forty minutes he had sub-dued the animal to the point of being able to mount him without having him buck.

The boy had caught a glimpse of the handsome stranger, and recognizing an audience, had done his best, as is the way with youth. The fellow's devil-may-care swagger had quite won him. As he left the corral, Ramon saw the man bow to him. Returning his greeting, he addressed the stranger.

"My compliments," the latter murmured. "From experience, I know that the proper breaking of a horse is solely a matter of touch,—an art in itself. Allow me to introduce myself, sir: I am Juan Montesoro, of Mexico City, dubbed Pancho for short, by those who know me."

"You honor me, sir," the boy replied. "I am Ramon, the eldest son of Don Fernando Gutierrez. I take it, you are a stranger in this land."

"I am, indeed! Was that piebald the last of the *remuda?*"

"No. We have some fifteen ahead of us, but only one a trouble-maker,—that gray with the lop ears."

Ramon wiped the perspiration from his face as he surveyed the animal about which he had just spoken. It was unbearably hot for so late in the year. The men had saddled another horse, and he raised clouds of dust as he tore, riderless, around the corral. A lariat swished through the air, and the horse went down. Vargas, the hacienda's best vaquero, was upon him when he reared erect.

This work was hard, dangerous, but these men

accepted it as an adventure. Vargas soon led his mount from the corral, and Ramon and Montesoro saw the lop-eared gray singled out for his turn. The boy voiced a foreboding grunt as he watched his men approach the horse.

"Is he so bad?" Montesoro asked.

"He threw the best of us yesterday afternoon. The horse has got the devil in him. But for a lucky leap, Vargas, our best man, would have been dashed to death against the fence "

Montesoro studied the gray for another minute. Then:

"I'll break that horse for you, if you'll permit me, Señor Gutierrez."

The offer came as so great a surprise to Ramon that he looked at the other dumbly for a second. At last:

"It is no easy task, señor. I wonder if you realize what a mistake would cost?"

Montesoro nodded his head. "I assure you, I am no fool. I have yet to see the horse that could throw me. Have I your permission?"

Ramon had half-hoped that the stranger would insist, for naturally he was human enough to want to see the mettle of this dashing *caballero*. As you wish," he answered, then: "I warn you, keep him away from the fence."

Vargas was none too well pleased at hearing that he was not to be given a chance to redeem himself for yesterday's fiasco. With bad grace he held the hat and jacket which Montesoro handed to him.

Four others got the gray into the corral and threw him. Montesoro shouted instructions as they struggled to put on a saddle. The feat was accomplished finally, and with a cry to stand clear, the stranger leaped to the gray's back.

Ramon had not underestimated the horse. Whirling, kicking, bucking, the gray careened around the corral. Straight up into the air he reared, and although the stranger ripped him with his spurs, he did not flatten out. But these were only parlor tricks. When they failed, the horse began bucking in earnest. He stood, stiff-legged, and bucked from the tip of his tail to the end of his nose, in whip-snapping, back-breaking lunges.

The rider held on, and shrieked to goad the horse further. Again and again the gray tried this. It availed nothing. The air grew so heavy with dust that man and beast were hidden from view temporarily. The horse snorted in rage. Up, and up, he reared, until even the wise Montesoro thought he was going over upon his back.

In a flash the horse came down, and like lightning, dashed for the fence. The gray's bloodshot eyes rolled. It was apparent that if he could not buck the man off, he would crush him to death against the fence. Ramon yelled for him to jump.

Vargas' lip curled. Now they would see the stuff of the man!

The stranger was alive to his danger. He made no effort to turn the horse; but instead, with grace and a flourish, he swung his inside leg over the pommel. The cinches were tight; the saddle held. The gray crashed into the fence and rocked from the impact. With a badly bruised shoulder for his trouble, he backed off, and like a charging bull tried it again. But the man's eye was too quick for the horse. Always, with a second to spare, he was free, and daring the animal to do its worst.

From plunging into the fence, the horse changed its tactics to racing alongside it, hoping to brush off his tormenter. With all of his mighty speed he dashed around the corral until he was winded. Panting and heaving, he came to a broken halt, his head swinging from side to side.

It became Montesoro's turn then. With quirt and spur he made the pace. Sweat and lather dripped from the gray. He was thoroughly beaten. But the man lashed him on. It was cruel!

Suzanna had returned to the scene of the horse-breaking astride a ragged-looking pony, daring with eyes and lips a repetition of the laughter with which the crowd had bidden her godspeed an hour before. The sight of the dashing cavalier, who outrode Don Fernando's vaqueros with seeming ease, caused her to eye her tomboy attire disparagingly.

Ramon had not seen Suzanna, so intently had he been watching the man in the corral. He held up his hand now for the stranger to stop. The gray was being punished needlessly. As the boy signaled, a shout of applause rang out; the rider had brought the horse to a slithering stand directly in front of where Suzanna sat her pony. With a sweep of his arm he bowed to the ground. The applause increased. Montesoro had used showmanship of a sort these emotional children could understand.

Vargas led away the gray. Suzanna shivered as she saw its torn, bleeding mouth. The stranger's horsemanship had awed her, but her eyes flashed now as the man stood before her smiling.

Montesoro had caught that flash of her eyes and the thought behind it. He grinned. He believed that nothing succeeded so well with women as a heavy hand. He assayed Suzanna more rapidly than other men had been wont to. He read the impudence in her tilted lips, the roguishness in her eyes, and because his experience with women was wide, he drew upon his ego to answer unhesitatingly many other questions about her. Enough, that she had seen him flay the horse. She would not forget that. And though evidently a peon, he found her very attractive.

"A girl could ride that gray, now," he said to her without further ado.

Suzanna was not slow to retort.

"Why did you break his heart?" she snapped. "Better that he run wild on the range than be the hang-dog he is now."

Montesoro smiled admiringly at her.

"No one has ever broken you—yet, have they?" he asked his question with all the intimacy he could put into his voice.

Suzanna laughed, but points of fire flared in her eyes. Tauntingly she said:

"Perhaps you would like to try, eh?"

The stranger did not put his answer into words, but he told himself that he knew the way of these hot-heads. Give them time and a free-hand, and they would come to book as easily as the shy and demure ones.

Ramon came up then, and his appearance put an end to the little scene. The boy had been impressed by the bit of skill and daring the tall stranger had shown. Glancing at him now, he saw him smiling, unruffled, and rather envied the man.

The boy was thoroughly annoyed with Suzanna for having ventured back to the corral, and without meeting her eyes he offered his arm to the stranger and led him toward his horse.

Suzanna bit her lips angrily at this, but someone had dislodged the coyote from his hiding place and she found amusement enough in the chase which followed to soon forget Ramon's treatment.

"I suppose you are bound for Monterey," the boy said to the stranger as they reached the roadside.

"Yes, eventually," the man declared. "California appeals to me. I rather expect to settle here."

"Well," Ramon exclaimed hospitably, "if you are in no great haste why not tarry awhile? Allow me to extend the courtesy of the hacienda to you. My father will make you most welcome."

Montesoro was quite moved by this show of friendship.

"You but prove the tales I have heard of California," he said graciously. "Where else in the New World would a stranger be shown such kindness? To a certainty, I should be much pleased to accept your hospitality. I trust I disarrange no plans of yours."

"Perish the thought. We see all too few new faces. Vargas can manage here; let us go on to the *caserio*. I presume you have friends somewhere in the province?"

"Only one; a lady whom I met in Mexico,—the charming daughter of Don Diego de Sola."

"Chiquita de Sola?" Ramon exclaimed questioningly, and in evident surprise.

"But of course you would know her," Montesoro declared. "A friar informed me this morning that your hacienda adjoined her father's rancho."

"Know her?" the boy said musingly. "Indeed! We have been betrothed since childhood."

It was Pancho Montesoro's turn to be surprised. Chiquita had never mentioned any such embarrassing entanglement to him. His eyes narrowed menacingly as he looked away. With a silent curse, he asked himself if he had made this trip for nothing. This boy's father was reputed to be one of the wealthiest men in California. How was he, a penniless adventurer, to compete with him?

He had counted most heavily on capturing the girl, and thereby gaining access to the De Sola fortune. He had been quite at ease, financially as well as otherwise, in Mexico City. Bull-fighting as a sport was yet to be introduced, in a professional way, in the Province. There was no work at hand for him here. Every plan he had made was lost to him if he failed to win Chiquita.

While the flirtation between them had ripened into love with the girl, Montesoro had only found her beautiful, interesting,—and a means to fortune. So while what Chiquita represented had become a matter of vital interest, the girl herself disturbed him not at all. He found it possible to hate her for having compromised him in this fashion.

"It's about what one should expect from an aristocrat," he muttered to himself, and so immeasurable was his ego that he saw nothing to smile at in his thought. But while Montesoro's chagrin was great, he was gambler enough to keep his emotion from the boy. With seeming sincerity he addressed himself to Ramon.

"You are to be congratulated," he said. "Your future wife is one of the most queenly women I have ever had the honor of knowing."

CHAPTER X

THE RULE OF A GENTLEMAN

Pancho Montesoro found life at the *Hacienda de Gutierrez* most pleasant. Don Fernando accepted him at face value, and Doña Luz saw in him only a most agreeable young man.

Suzanna had not left for the Mission as yet, and she found opportunities for comparing the man with Ramon and the bold Pérez. The newcomer suffered but little in this. Her inexperienced eyes being quite dazzled by his graces. Whenever he smiled at her, little chills raced down her spine. She seemed caught up and drawn to him. Several times she had almost obeyed the impulse; but, unsophisticated as she was, intuition whispered to her to beware of the fellow. Being a woman, Suzanna's curiosity quite outweighed her caution, and she alternately advanced and retreated in the flirtation Montesoro connived to keep alive.

On the fourth night of his stay at the hacienda, he strolled in the shadows of the servants' patio, thrumming his guitar. The hour was so late that he openly dared this loss of caste.

Suzanna, wrapped in her mantilla, sat in the deeper shadow of the doorway which led into the granary. She saw him pass without suspecting her presence. Her first impulse was to call him, and she half-raised her hand, only to let it drop again, caution bidding her beware.

The decision was taken from her, however, for as slight as her movement had been, the man had noticed it, and turning, he sat down upon the step below her.

He rolled a cigarette in silence, feeling sure that he impressed her with the intimacy of the situation by his very lack of speech. The cigarette lighted, he leaned towards her, and looking up into her face with veiled eyes, he whispered:

"*Mi corazón palpita per tí; no oyes?*" his hand closing over hers.

It was a pretty speech: "My heart throbs for you; can't you hear?"

Suzanna had always found love most pleasant, but her throat went dry now, as his flesh touched hers. With an effort she murmured:

"*Cállate!* Someone will hear."

Montesoro continued to gaze at her intently, drinking his fill of her excitement. With nothing short of artistry he turned from her and picked up his guitar and struck off into a lilting melody.

His keen ears caught the uneasy sigh which escaped her lips as the song ended. Suzanna made to rise, but his strong arm reached out and caught her around the waist.

"Do I sing so illy, little bird?" he whispered.

" 'Tis late," Suzanna protested as she fought to disengage his arm.

The man smiled at her effort, and pulling himself up a step so that he sat beside her, he plucked a rose from a bush which twined about the door, and chucked her under the chin with it. Involuntarily, Suzanna turned up her face so that her lips were close to his. Before she could recover, he drew her close to him and held her helpless.

"Thou most beautiful girl in the world," he murmured. "Thine eyes are as the most precious stones; thy hair as sheer as finest silk; thy brow fairer than any gentle sun or whispering wind ever kissed. Thy lips are more perfect than a cupid's bow, more colorful than a pomegranate."

It was his favorite love-speech. Chiquita de

Sola had answered to the tug of it. Surely this poor peon could not deny its appeal. Great was his suprise, then, to see Suzanna's dark, lustrous eyes molten with rage.

"What, *amor mia*, you are angry? You who I liken unto a rose blooming in a dark corner of some remote rancho, with only an occasional kiss from the kindly sun? True, you bloom, but not half so fully as you would did the sun but kiss you continually."

"Yes; but a rose continually kissed by the sun soon withers and dies," Suzanna exclaimed vehemently. "Unhand me!"

"Think you then that the sun would not distemper his rays did you but come within his vision? No, no, *querida!* You are out of place here. Mexico City with its beautiful gardens, its bowers, its gay life, its bull-fights,—there do you belong, Suzanna—with me!"

"So?" a voice boomed in unctious sweetness as its owner stepped forth from his concealment in back of the flower garden. "Your tongue is very glib, señor; but I am constrained to doubt its veracity."

Montesoro taken at such a mean advantage, released Suzanna and got to his feet stealthily. Too many times in his checkered career had he extricated himself from like circumstance to be discountenanced now. The man before him was a stranger, but undoubtedly a jealous lover. Pancho knew how to impress his sort. A show of prowess had opened the way more than once. So, apparently without design, he drew his knife, and singling out a moonlight tipped rosebud which clung to a post some fifteen feet distant, he flipped his blade toward it and pierced the flower to the heart.

The intruder turned his face then so that the light caught it. Suzanna gasped as she recognized the bandit, Benito Pérez. The outlaw smiled at her as he caught sight of her tear-filled eyes.

"*No llores,*—don't cry—little one," he reassured her. The braggadocio and challenge of Montesoro's act was not lost on the bandit. He had lived too long in Old Spain not to realize its significance. And yet, with the greatest indifference, he turned his back on the man, and moving so that the distance between himself and the post was much greater, he drew his knife and sent it whistling through the air, nor waited to see the quality of his aim. A dull thud followed as the knife struck and pierced the hilt of the other's weapon.

With varying degrees of emotion Pancho and Suzanna gazed at the quivering knives.

"Señor," Pérez said in tones which carried the chilling coldness of death, "the inviolate rule of a gentleman is never to take advantage of his position as one. You are a guest here."

"More than I dare you can say," Montesoro answered angrily. "I haven't the *honor* of your acquaintance."

"For your surmise," Pérez muttered, "—it is correct. I am here without invitation. And certain it is that I would honor you in giving you acquaintance. I am Benito Pérez!"

"The outlaw?" Pancho questioned unbelievingly.

"Of my many titles it is the one I like the least; but I do not deny it."

"Now that you have turned protector," the toreador said surlily, "you can add another to your long list. You have had good care to stay clear of me as I have ridden about the rancho properly armed."

"True," Pérez grinned. "Wasted effort ever galled me. I have no time for empty pockets. Allow me, now, to bid you good-night."

Pérez lifted a hand toward the casa. Montesoro snarled an oath at what he knew to be a command. "It grows late," the robber-captain cautioned. The syllables clicked off his tongue. Pancho hesitated no longer.

When he was gone, the bandit turned to Suzanna. "And you, little one, art surprised to find me Pérez?"

"Your mogador betrayed you," she answered. "Much ado I had explaining how I came by it. But your coming here—are you mad?"

"You hold the act so rash, then?"

"Doubly so, now. That coward will raise a cry against you. The pack will be upon you!"

"And yet I do not flee," Pérez said softly. "I have had tales of this *torero*. He convicts himself! His words are as empty as his purse. He does well to mock me with the word 'protector.' Is there no one here to see through the man? I am afraid for you."

Suzanna stared at him speechlessly at this show of solicitude in her behalf.

"Truly," she said when she had regained the use of her tongue, "you almost make me forget that when last we met you, yourself, were none too mindful of my innocence. Hast our robber turned friar?"

Suzanna did not see the man's mouth set or the look of sadness which crept into his eyes as he bowed his head. The next instant, however, Suzanna's fingers gripped the man's arm. Pérez had snapped erect. A cry had rang out from the casa:

"Socorro!—Help—*El bandido Pérez!"*

"Go at once!" Suzanna urged excitedly. "A dozen men will answer him."

"First, I shall see you safe from gossip. Hasten while I hold the ladder."

Stairways were a luxury confined at this early date to the houses of the masters. The workers on the hacienda ascended to their quarters above the granary by ladder. Pérez steadied the one which the girl used, and half-lifting her, he set her upon a rung waist-high with himself and sent her scrambling upward. But she had not reached the window which led into her room before the outlaw heard himself hailed, and turning, he found Ramon facing him.

"It *is* you, then!" the boy cried. "Stand ready to defend yourself!"

Ramon had been the first to answer Pancho's cry

and hear his story. Bidding his guest wait to direct the others to the scene, the boy had dashed into the patio. Pérez did not raise his voice as he addressed him.

"For my presence here, you shall have whatever satisfaction you may demand; but not until this child is safe from the scandal mongering tongues of those who soon will be here. For, peon or not, I hold that she is a lady. Would you have her made party to a brawl?"

Ramon had not forgotten the taunts Pérez had tossed at him the day of the attack on the wagon, nor had he forgiven the man for his attentions to Suzanna. Hot anger had consumed him upon finding them together here in the patio of his own home.

He cooled perceptibly as he saw Pérez wave Suzanna on. The man's words were not in keeping with the conduct Montesoro had accused him of in his hurried tale. Ramon felt rebuffed,—a crude lout, whereas the man before him bore himself as a cavalier.

Not until Suzanna had stepped through the window did the outlaw turn to the boy. Ramon had caught the sound of hurrying feet and he knew that in another minute the patio would be overflow-ing with men. Pérez had drawn his sword and stood ready to defend himself. Surely the man could not be deaf to that sound of scurrying feet. And yet, he waited with seeming unconcern for the boy to raise his blade.

"You are more the don than I," Ramon said to him. "I bow my head in shame that it was neces-sary for you to remind me of my conduct as a gentleman. Lower your weapon and go."

"What a lad!" Pérez murmured to himself as he gazed at Ramon. He made to turn, then, toward the arch which led to the road, but as he did so Pancho and the others confronted him.

Without hesitation, Ramon leaped to the rob-ber's side. "Stand back!" he cried. "This man goes untouched."

"Is he not Pérez, the bandit?" Pancho demanded. "You do not mean that you are going to allow such a rich prize to slip through your fingers?"

"He goes free!" Ramon repeated.

Montesoro drew back dumfounded. A surprised murmur broke from the others, also. The boy walked toward them, and as he did so, he came face to face with the knives the two men had thrown. A question in his eyes, he looked at Pérez.

"The one in your hand is mine," the outlaw admitted.

He reached out for it as Ramon offered it to him.

"And this other one, imbedded in the post,—how came it here?"

Pérez paused before he replied. The crowd had caught the question and waited for the answer.

"Perhaps your guest will enlighten you," he drawled provokingly. And then, stiffly erect, he marched to the gate and was gone.

CHAPTER XI

A HOUSE IS PUT IN ORDER

THE effect of this affair was to cast a shadow over the heretofore smiling hacienda. Suzanna refused—absolutely—to tell Ramon what had happened, and his guest not volunteering any information, the boy felt constrained not to insist.

Don Fernando had received a very unsatisfactory account of the bandit's visit, and he sensed that something moved under the surface in connection with the episode.

Suspicion is always an excellent instrument of torture, and it proved itself so in this instance. Fortunately, the following day brought news of great moment to all at the *Rancho de Gutierrez,*— Don Diego, his daughter and their retinue of servants were returning!

They were but a day's journey away to the south at present. The post-rider who brought word from them had passed their coach at Santa Barbara.

Don Fernando and Doña Luz could not have received more agreeable information. A hundred tasks presented themselves immediately. Their friend's house must be put in order after these years of accumulating dust. Delicacies must be purchased in Monterey for the sumptuous dinner with which their friends should be greeted. Their own house, though spotless now, must needs be gone over painstakingly, for such is the way of human beings.

Those things pertaining to her own home, the flowers, and foods to be prepared, Doña Luz saw to. Ruiz, as major-domo of the hacienda, transmitted Don Fernando's orders to his servants.

Ruiz received the news of their neighbors' return with a sour face. He had been quite in accord with his master regarding Suzanna's education and her enforced absence from the hacienda. The old man was not blind to Ramon's interest in the girl, and he half-suspected the real reason lying beneath Don Fernando's magnanimous offer to Suzanna. The unexpected return of Don Diego and his daughter was very likely to upset these plans.

Immediately after giving his orders in the scullery and truck garden, Ruiz sought Suzanna. He found her watching Ramon, who was busily engaged in braiding a horsehair *reata.* The old man bowed to his young master and then spoke to the girl.

"Get a jug and brooms," he ordered, "and follow me."

"But why, father?" Suzanna demanded, loth to leave.

"Ask no questions," Ruiz answered sharply, annoyed at this impertinence before the boy. "There is work in plenty to be done before to-morrow."

Some half-dozen servants laden with brooms and other utensils entered the compound at this instant, and catching sight of them, Suzanna's eyes widened.

"What are we to do?" she asked.

"Don Diego and his family return to-morrow," Ruiz replied sharply. "His house is to be cleaned and aired. Come, we have little time to waste."

Suzanna and Ramon stared at each other in mute surprise at this news. The boy's face fell as comprehension came to him. Something akin to terror filled Suzanna's eyes.

"Coming home—to-morrow!" she gasped.

Ruiz ignored her and said to Ramon:

"Your father had word by post-rider not half an hour ago. The news must fill you with happiness."

"Why?" Ramon snapped sullenly.

"*La Señorita de Sola*, your betrothed——"

"A good servant minds his own business, Ruiz," Ramon warned.

Ruiz took the rebuff in silence. Turning to the waiting servants, he waved them on, and then said to Suzanna:

"See that you follow us immediately."

The boy and the girl looked at each other dumbly when they were alone. Both felt that they had reached a crisis in their lives. As the days had passed without further word of her going to San Luis Bautista, Suzanna had allowed the ultimatum to rest lightly upon her head. Womanlike she had been able to distill rare pleasure from the embroglio in which Ramon and Pancho had confronted Pérez. She realized now that golden days had slipped by her which she could have shared with the boy. She berated herself for having cast eyes at Montesoro. Pérez, she was forced to admit, interested her, but it was not because of love for him.

Love? What a strange thing it was! She had looked forward to love as a rightful heritage of her sex. Love to her had meant happiness, a gladness of heart and body; yet misery, such as she had heard dogs voice, was in her soul. And yet, with womanly instinct she knew this thing was love. The thought crushed her and dimmed her eyes with tears. The Holy Mother's name escaped her lips as she asked herself why she had been born; the tragedy of life spreading out before her endlessly.

In a flash of understanding the girl saw just how wide was the gulf which separated this man from her. To-morrow, a woman who was his equal in everything the world set store by, would come to take her place at his side. What chance had she, a poor, uneducated peon, beside her?

Ramon almost followed her train of thought, and the hot blood of youth flaring up in him, he was minded to take her and flee. Chiquita de Sola was less than the dust to him. Suzanna held the culmination of every desire he had known. What did riches and caste matter? This was a new world,—a new land—men were done with the cant of kings and friars. California was the land of opportunity, of freedom,—a man's future was what he wished to make it.

Answering this urge, Ramon stepped toward Suzanna, eyes flashing, his arms outstretched.

"O, Blessed Mother of God," she muttered in despair as she sensed the meaning of those outstretched arms. The desire to rest within their embrace but for a second overcame her, but even as she made her decision, Don Fernando walked into the compound.

Ramon's teeth sank into his lips as he saw her turn away without a word and enter the house. His arms fell to his sides, as he stood there stunned.

Don Fernando preferred not to recognize the meaning of the scene he had interrupted. As though he were conveying a surprise, he acquainted his son with the fact of Don Diego's return.

"Yes, yes, Ruiz informed me," the boy replied, going back to his task dejectedly.

"Your mother wants you to go to Monterey for certain dainties," his father continued. "Do you prefer to leave now, or this afternoon?"

"As mother prefers," Ramon answered. "I shall be through with this in a few minutes."

Suzanna came out and trudged across the road in the wake of the other servants as father and son talked. Their brief conversation at an end, Don Fernando followed her.

His face was severe as he entered the house of his friend. A sadness, which wholly obliterated the joy that Don Diego's home-coming had brought, rested upon him. How stupid he had been not to have packed off Suzanna at once to San Luis Bautista. Well, she should go before Chiquita arrived, train or not.

Ruiz had busied himself in the kitchen, leaving part of the servants to put the other rooms of the large house in order. When Suzanna entered, she had found them more intent on play than work. For once, she had no desire to abet them. The merriment ended most abruptly as Señor Gutierrez strode into the living-room, his face red with rage. Suzanna saw him glance at her, and knowing that from past experience he would blame her for this loitering, she got to her feet and ran toward the altar-room. There Don Fernando found her.

The girl had heard him follow her, and realizing that his wrath was to be visited on her, she sank to her knees and assumed an attitude of penitent prayer.

Don Fernando waited for her to finish her devotions. Suzanna exhausted her words of prayer before she arose to face him.

"Child," he said sternly. "I am weary of your pranks. We have little enough time to arrange for my friend's arrival, and yet you countenance—and I vow instigated—such conduct as greeted me when I entered this house. You are demoralizing every servant on the hacienda."

"I have been guilty so often that my innocence this once is unbelievable, I know," Suzanna said sadly. "You have been too indulgent."

Don Fernando looked at her shrewdly. Truly this was a new Suzanna. Overjoyed to find her so tractable, he made to inform her at once that she went to the Mission at sunrise.

Amazed, Suzanna heard him out. Horror transfixed her face as he finished.

"But I have no desire for an education," she said with choking voice. "Please—I do not want to leave here, Don Fernando. I should die were you to send me away from this hacienda where I know every flower and blade of grass. I have been so happy here. I will work, oh, so hard,—you will have no cause to find fault with me if you will but let me stay. Please, I beg you."

Suzanna's emotion engulfed her. With a sob she sank to her knees, her tears blinding her as she looked up at her master.

"Don't send me away from you, from Doña Luz, from Ramon—from my father," she implored. "Oh, oh,—I cannot go. Everything that I know and—and—love is here. I—I won't go! I can't!"

"But you must," Don Fernando declared firmly, but not unkindly. "The time will pass quickly enough. You be ready to go at sunrise. Guara, the Indian, shall accompany you."

Suzanna continued to plead with him, but the determined old man remained firm in his decision. Don Fernando left her to compose herself in the quietness of this holy room. Upon leaving, he pulled the door to, and Suzanna, alone with her grief, threw herself upon the cold flagging before the altar and sobbed piteously.

An hour later she dragged herself to her room. She had stopped her tears. Her anger, too, had subsided. Resignation, hopeless and cold had taken its place. It took but a short time to gather

her meager belongings and make them ready against the morrow's journey. Saying good-by to Timoteo, and Chichi, the bear, proved a much harder task.

Chichi had an affectionate disposition and he hugged her with his hairy paws as Suzanna petted him and whispered little love words in his ears.

The girl saw much alike in their situations. She was Don Fernando's chattel just as Chichi was hers. The bear was petted and humored; but a steel chain around his neck marked his movements for him. The sight of the chain filled Suzanna with rage. Within her blazed a sudden hatred for all that was tyrannical and oppressive.

Dropping to her knees, she unfastened the chain, and led the bear to a field in back of the barns.

"Run, Chichi," she exclaimed. "Go back to your hills and your woods. Far better that some chance hunter should kill you than that you stay here to be ordered about as I am ordered. Go, *jovencito*, before my father catches you."

The bear showed no disposition to embrace his freedom, and although Suzanna beat him with a stick, he but circled round and round her feet. The girl shook her head sadly as she realized that the poor brute's affection for her outweighed his desire to return to the wild.

Suzanna had heard her father calling her, and he approached now. He saw enough of her purpose with the bear to anger him. Grabbing the chain from her, he snapped it around the animal's neck.

Don Fernando had communicated his wishes to Ruiz, and the girl's father had readily agreed to his master's plans. The peon was a good servant and he never questioned the orders of his superiors. In this instance, however, he saw the calamity that he had feared, safely averted by what his master proposed. And that, too, for reasons which would have surprised Don Fernando.

Suzanna knew better than to hope that Ruiz would go counter to Don Fernando's wishes. When she spoke to her father it was only to ask him if he had been informed of what the morrow held.

"Of course. Have you packed your things?"

"I have," Suzanna answered dully. "Does Ramon know that I am leaving?"

"He is on his way to Monterey. I do not know whether his father informed him or not. You give your question a pointing which implies that your leaving is of importance to our young master. Again I tell you that you presume. You would do well to keep your eyes to your own kind. Doña Luz has set out some clothes and trinkets for you. Go to her and thank her as she deserves. And if it pleases you, give a hand in the kitchen until the bell rings, for I know you have some skill with cakes."

Suzanna found that the news of her departure for San Luis Bautista was common property in the kitchen. Caridad and the other women saw in it but another manifestation of the great goodness of their master, and were frankly jealous of the grand journey ahead of Suzanna.

The girl looked at them hopelessly. What better could one expect from such fools, she asked herself. Suzanna was glad when Doña Luz sent for her. Better it was to be misunderstood by your superiors than by your equals!

With an armful of things from *la señora's* precious store, Suzanna crossed the patios to her quarters as the evening bell sounded. As she did so, Pancho Montesoro rode in. He had been away from the house since early morning, and Suzanna's old spirit flamed for a brief second as she beheld the man. Naturally, he could not know that Chiquita de Sola was returning to-morrow. Suzanna resolved that he should be informed immediately, and by her in a manner best suited to embarrass him.

Montesoro swung to the ground in front of her a minute later.

"Well," he grinned. "What is the meaning of this? Art getting married?"

"From what do you infer that?" Suzanna answered saucily, "——my face or this armful of clothes?"

"I but jested," Pancho said ingratiatingly. "For the first time, I find you looking sad and blue. Meet me to-night and let me put a smile upon your pretty face."

"You are so sure you could?"

"Don't taunt me," he muttered dramatically. "You know that my heart and soul are yours alone. I should die were you to be taken away from me."

Miserable though she was, Suzanna could smile at this bald lying.

"Death hovers near you, then, my dashing lord," she assured him. "I leave for San Luis Bautista at sunrise."

"Oh, no—no!" the rascal exclaimed, still the actor.

"It is all too true," Suzanna replied firmly. "But"—and mischief fairly twinkled in her eyes —"do not pine. One arrives to-morrow who will busily engage thee."

"Yes?" Pancho queried.

"Your friend, Chiquita de Sola! She arrives at noon."

The man staggered, so great was his surprise. Suzanna felt well repaid. Peon she might be, but she had thrown the name of a lady of high degree into this man's face when his words of love to her were still warm upon his lips.

Montesoro saw that she had played with him, and he hated her for it.

"What is it that you insinuate?" he demanded hotly. *"La Señorita de Sola* has my most profound respect."

Suzanna mocked him with a courtesy.

"I wonder," she murmured pointedly, "if you have her father's."

The girl continued across the patio without waiting for an answer. She knew she had drawn blood. The man's face was livid as her trailing laugh floated across the garden. Impotent, he stood there and cursed her beneath his breath. With pleasure, he could have shaken the life out of her.

Suzanna's elation was short-lived. Supper proved a grim jest, and to escape from those who sought to fill her with advice, she sought refuge in her room. Sleep, however, was impossible. Later, when she did doze off, a great ogre chased her in her dreams. Round and round the rancho, he pursued her. Her cries for help went unanswered, until at last, the ogre forced her into his cave. There, she saw Ramon, but his hands were chained. Soon, the ogre had her a captive likewise, and then he removed his masque. It was Don Fernando! With a cruel laugh he turned and left them. Suzanna heard the giant stones in the entrance falling into place and knew that nothing but slow, lingering death faced them.

The girl tossed on her bed as her tortured brain continued to plumb the horrors of the ogre's cave. Wet with perspiration, she sat up in answer to her father's summons. The first hint of dawn was in the sky.

"Come," Ruiz repeated. "It is morning. Time for a bite, and Guara will be ready with the horses."

Ruiz descended to the kitchen and prepared a scant repast. The Indian joined him, and when Suzanna came down, the three sat in silence and ate. The great kitchen was still dark. Shadows clothed the master's house. In the patios the flowers and vines were wet with dew. Everything was still; even the birds. Fresh, pungent, earthy odors and aromas filled the nostrils. The new-born day was pregnant with the riches the night had stored up for it.

But it was strange, unreal to Suzanna. This stillness, which made one talk in whispers; this lethargy, which held even the leaves motionless, had no part in the hacienda she knew. Dumbly she followed her father and the Indian to where the horses stood.

Ruiz was not an emotional man, but he caressed the girl before he lifted her into the saddle. Affection from him was so unlooked for that it unnerved Suzanna. As from a distance she heard Ruiz telling her not to cry. The horses were moving, then. Her father opened the gate, and Guara and she passed from the patio to the highroad.

Less than a mile away they came to the hills. The Indian, mindful of the cool hours still at hand, urged his horses down the descent into the next valley.

"Hold!" Suzanna cried to him. "From this spot I take my last look for two years at the *Hacienda de Gutierrez*. Do not be impatient, Guara. I want to wait here until the sun touches the *caserio*. It will be but a minute."

The Indian grunted a grudging consent. And so, from her saddle, Suzanna said farewell to the only home she had ever known.

CHAPTER XII

GUARA pushed the horses without let up during the early morning. Don Fernando had given him most definite instructions as to his conduct. The Indian intended reaching Los Pinos by high-noon for a short siesta. Evening should find them at Paso Robles. An early start the following morning, then, would see them at the Mission by noon. Guara had no mind to be absent from the *fiesta* which would most certainly follow the return of Don Diego to his hacienda. When once Suzanna was off his hands, the Indian knew that he could ride, without pause, the intervening miles between himself and the *caserio*, excepting the minute or two in which to water his pony.

Even though the girl was saddle-wise, she complained at the pace Guara set. But Guara was deaf to her complaints. They should rest at Los Pinos by noon, and it followed that when the sun reached its zenith they rode into the cooling shade of the pines at the springs of Los Pinos.

Suzanna had heard of the life and color which flowed along *El Camino Real*. So far she had seen nothing but sun-burnt hills, wide, parched valleys and unending stretches of dust-covered road. Therefore, she was quite unprepared for the reception which greeted her as she rode into the shelter of the trees. Before her reclined at least a score of men clad in the blue and red uniforms of Mexico. It was obviously, a detachment of troops on its way to the Presidio at Monterey. The officer in charge, a loose-lipped lieutenant overly brave in his display of gold lace, smiled at her ingratiatingly, but not until his sensuous eyes had properly appraised this morsel which the saints had sent hither to break the monotony of this God-forsaken country.

Suzanna shared her master's contempt for most things Mexican. Still, it was not her hatred of Mexican officialdom which made her lips curl scornfully as she faced this young subaltern. The look in the man's eyes made this encounter a matter of personal hatred. Suzanna saw that Guara was little pleased at having stumbled into this hornet's nest.

Mexican soldiery had a little way of silencing an offending Indian. Guara was alive to the main chance, and he told himself that it would be very, very unwise to offend these miserable señors. Suzanna, however, was of sterner stuff. To rest here was but courting trouble. With a toss of her head, she turned and addressed her Indian guide.

"Guara," she said evenly, "our horses have quenched their thirst. Let us be on our way."

The lieutenant reached for her bridle at that.

"But, pretty one," he said with a fine show of feeling, "where does one journey to that she can afford to turn her back on the cooling shade of this enticing spot?"

"The Mexican government having no word of me," Suzanna answered tartly, "I presume my answer to be none of your business."

The officer was not abashed by this.

"You force me to make it my business, now," he said insinuatingly. "Here is food and drink,— do I seem so ill in your eyes that you disdain to break bread with me?" He caught Suzanna's wrist as she glared at him. "Come, now. You are going to repay my hospitality with a smile. Four weeks have we been on our way, without a pretty face to rest my eyes. They are hungry to feast upon the loveliness of one so beautiful as you."

The officer's men were keenly interested in what went on before them. They were all low fellows, the most of them but lately free of some prison. They voiced a ruffianly laugh as they saw Suzanna lift her hand and roundly slap the lieutenant's face.

Their ribald laughter infuriated him a great deal more than did the smack which this pretty girl gave him. The man had but little power over his men, but even so, that little trembled in the balance now. Realizing that he played for a larger stake than the favor of this peon, he determined to waste no further time. Jerking her arm savagely, he pulled Suzanna so far forward that she lost her balance and almost fell into his embrace.

Guara sat his horse unmoved; he knew that a dozen pairs of eyes watched him, daring him to betray even the slightest interest in what went on before him.

The laugh with which the young officer had received his burden was short-lived, for Suzanna became a scratching, clawing fiend. He tried to hide his face from her nails, by covering it with his arms as he unhanded her and stepped back.

Suzanna was after him as quickly as Timoteo had taken after Miguel's cowardly rooster.

And now, although Suzanna would have been equally in danger with any single one of them, the soldiers became her supporters, and cheered her on to further indignities upon their leader. For the lieutenant, the incident became a catastrophe. And then, when he was seen at his very worst, a coach-and-four wheeled around a curve in the road and came to a dizzy halt before him.

The mein of the gentleman who leaped to the ground and faced him belligerently, as well as the costly trappings of the splendid coach, said all too plainly that here was a man of some estate. That a girl of ripe beauty, the man's daughter no doubt, was a passenger within the coach and pulled the curtains now and studied him coldly, did not lesson the lieutenant's embarrassment.

"What play is this we have here?" the owner of the carriage demanded hastily.

At the sound of his voice, Suzanna screamed.

"Don Diego!" she repeated again and again. And seeing that recognition of herself did not come to Don Diego's eyes, she said eagerly, her body trembling with emotion:

"Don't you remember little Suzanna?"

"Suzanna?" Don Diego gasped. "No? It isn't —it can't be little tomboy Suzanna?"

"But don't you see that it is,—that you find me unchanged, thanks to this beast, here."

Señor de Sola came close to the girl's side, and seeing that she was indeed his godchild, the daughter of his friend Fernando's Ruiz, he caught her to him and kissed her paternally.

"Child, child," he murmured, "you have grown into a beautiful woman. But tell me, what is the meaning of this scene?"

Don Diego heard her out with some impatience. Turning on the soldier he said:

"I have heard tales of outrages here in California, but I, with many others in the city, have had a habit of believing less than half of the rumors which we heard. It is plain they were not fabrications after all. You will have good cause to regret your action to-day. But for men of your type, we would hear no talk of separatists in California. You serve your country most illy, and the Presidio shall be so informed. And now, with what courtesy you can muster, withdraw yourself and your men to such a distance that I may converse freely with this child."

The power of wealth and social position was as great in that distant day as it is now, and the lieutenant soon removed his command to the corral among the trees where their horses awaited their pleasure.

"This Indian is with you, eh?" Don Diego exclaimed when they were alone. "But whither are you bound? You are a full thirty leagues from home."

"I am being sent away," Suzanna answered mournfully.

"Sent away?" Señor de Sola queried. "To where, and for what reason?"

"To the Mission San Luis Bautista," the girl replied. "I am to be educated."

"And does that make you so unhappy, child?" asked Don Diego.

"The very thought of it strangles me. It is like being sent away to prison. I shall die so far from all that I love. Don Fernando tries to help me, I know. But what is a peon to do with an education?"

Truly, this was a question not easily answered.

Don Diego chose to put it aside, and instead of answering it, he demanded brusquely:

"Does your master know how miserable your going makes you? He is a kind, just man, less stern than most. He evidently must believe he moves to please you in this thing."

"Oh, no, no," Suzanna murmured, her eyes filling with tears as her mind went back to the scene in the altar room of Don Diego's home. "Don Fernando knows that my heart is breaking."

"There, there," Don Diego said sympathetically as Suzanna's tears got the better of her. He was a sorely puzzled gentleman at the present moment, and for reasons which may not be apparent to those not familiar with the customs of Latin countries, and of California, of this period, in particular.

Don Diego and the peon Ruiz were *compadres,* —a relation between a child's own father and its godfather which was regarded as more sacred than any that blood alone could convey. Among peons and the lower classes this feeling ran so strongly as to often induce a man to name his own brother as his *compadre* so that their relation to each other should be even more intimate and sacred.

Usually, the godfather was in a position to dispense favors, and a man of Don Diego's standing would have many *ahijados* (godsons). Especially was this true in the rural country. More than once Indians have been known to die willingly for their *compadres*. Being a *padrino* (godfather) incurred responsibilities which no worthy man would shirk. A father could die with the perfect assurance that his *compadre* would care for his son or daughter with devotion equal to his own.

Understanding this, it is easy to see that by the very sacredness of the relation between godfather and child that the godfather acquired almost paternal control of the latter. The aristocrats, as well as the poorer classes, respected this. Of all Spanish institutions it was one of the noblest, and yet, it sometimes led to embarrassing situations. Don Diego found himself facing such a one at present.

Suzanna, as Ruiz daughter, belonged to his friend Gutierrez. That was the plain intent of peonage. Don Fernando, therefore, was well within his rights, according to custom, in ordering the girl about as he desired. Don Diego, as Suzanna's *padrino,* had the right to protest whenever he felt that his godchild got less than her deserts. He could even go so far as to pay Don Fernando a sum, which would equal Suzanna's debt to the *Hacienda de Gutierrez,* and become her master.

This procedure was often resorted to, but the question of friendship entered here. And Don Diego was loath to do ought which would offend the head of the house to which his daughter was betrothed.

"You have not offended Don Fernando or Doña Luz, have you?" Don Diego asked seeking for the reason which had led to the girl's exile.

"Not Doña Luz," Suzanna replied. "These clothes I have on, she gave me but last evening. But Don Fernando says I have demoralized every servant he has by my pranks,—and laziness."

"Oh, so that's it," Señor de Sola exclaimed, remembering the tomboy girl Suzanna had been, and finding in her words the real reason for Don Fernando's conduct. "Work ever was distasteful to you, child. If I take you back, will you show by your conduct that you have learned your lesson?"

"Oh, can I go back?" Suzanna asked eagerly, grasping Don Diego's hand in her excitement.

Moved by this show of affection, Señor de Sola had not the heart to deny her.

"You can, if you will give over your mischievous ways. I have as little time for pranks and laziness as my good friend Gutierrez."

The significance of this speech was not lost on Suzanna.

"You mean that I am to go to your hacienda?" she asked breathlessly.

"I will arrange it. My daughter has need of a maid. Señor Gutierrez will not be stubborn when he learns that she has decided on having you."

Suzanna's head whirled at this good news. Don Fernando might be powerful and able to order the lives of his servants as he willed; but here was her champion,—a man equally strong in his ways. The poor girl turned adoring eyes upon her savior as the full import of his marvelous intervention in her behalf sank into her consciousness.

"Let us go back to the coach," Don Diego suggested. "You can ride with us. My daughter will be glad to see you again, and pleased that I have found one whom she knows to be her maid."

Chiquita had been an interested observed of the little scene between her father and Suzanna. She

found the girl grown quite beautiful, but without
any sense of dress or style, judged by the standards
which she allowed herself. But as critical as she
was, Chiquita had to admit that Suzanna had little
of the peon about her. With an amused smile,
she saw her father and the girl start toward the
coach.

"Chiquita, don't you remember little Suzanna?"
Don Diego asked when he had opened the carriage door.

Chiquita's reply was an indifferent nod to the
girl.

Suzanna stood somewhat in awe of the fine
young lady before her. Her own clothes were
mean in comparison. And too, she was not slow
to see the superior manner with which Don Diego's
daughter greeted her. The two girls were of an
age and had spent many of their childhood hours
together. Here was a time for unbending for old
time's sake; but Suzanna searched Chiquita's face
in vain for the least sign of good-will or came-
raderie. She sensed that the other saw in her but
a peon, and that it was Chiquita's intention that she
should know it.

Poor Suzanna's heart sank at the thought of

having to serve her. For a second she almost wished that she had not asked to go back. As lonely and miserable as San Luis Bautista might prove it could be no worse than dancing attendance on this haughty girl who came home only to take Ramon away from her.

Don Diego took no heed of her wavering.

"Suzanna is going back with us," he went on. "She will make you an excellent maid."

"But Don Fernando?" Chiquita queried, not displeased at the thought of having Suzanna so squarely set in her place.

"I will arrange the matter with him," the girl's father replied. He directed Suzanna to get into the coach, and with an order to the Indian to follow, the horses were started.

Don Diego asked many questions as the heavy carriage rocked back and forth on its leather straps. Suzanna's interest in them overcame her fears and she was soon chattering like a magpie.

The coach was over-due by several hours when it came within sight of those waiting at the hacienda. A cry went up as it wheeled into view. The rest of the journey was down-hill, and the tired horses, scenting water and rest, bore away with a burst of speed.

Ramon had returned from Monterey to find Suzanna gone. Don Fernando had been hard put to stop the boy from racing after her. The incident had so upset the elder Gutierrez that he glanced uneasily at Ramon now, dreading to find the boy still sulking, with Don Diego and his daughter almost upon them.

What he read in the boy's expression gave him small comfort. Ramon was in a beastly temper. The holiday air of those about him but angered him more. He knew what was expected of him,— the fatuous greetings, the extravagant compliments, and the proper sort of pride in his wife-to-be.

God! how he hated it. Hot rebellion surged within him as he saw himself welcoming Chiquita de Sola while the girl whom he loved was miles away to the south, miserable and alone, save for a worthless Indian.

Pancho Montesoro, resplendent and debonair, lounged into the patio as the boy brooded. The sight of the man but added fuel to the fire raging in Ramon's brain. The fellow's impudence toward Suzanna still smarted. He had long since worn out his welcome, and had he been of thinner skin, he would not have asked for plainer evidence of the fact.

Pancho was quite pleased with himself over the turn events had taken. For one thing, Suzanna was beyond babbling to Chiquita. He had been at the hacienda so long that he did not fear that Don Diego would look upon him with suspicion. Hence, he could meet Chiquita without embarrassment. He felt very sure of himself as far as she was concerned. In fact, of all those gathered to greet the coach, Pancho Montesoro felt most certain of himself.

A cry broke from the lips of the crowd as the carriage swung into the patio. The servants, burdened with armfuls of flowers rushed forward as the driver brought his horses to a halt. A second later the door of the carriage opened, and as if by pre-arranged plan, the servitors of Don Fernando let loose a shower of blossoms which almost covered the person alighting from the coach. The surprise of this reception forced a thoroughly feminine cry from the startled recipient.

The crowd's excitement subsided abruptly as it sensed a familiar note. Don Fernando and Doña

Luz caught it, also. Pancho, Ruiz, Ramon—they looked at one another in surprise. And then, as the blossoms ceased falling, they saw Suzanna standing before them.

Ramon shouldered his way to her side, and not too soon either; his father being scarcely a step behind him.

The sight of the girl sent a hush over the assemblage. In that day, news was scarce, an incidents which would ordinarly go unnoticed because of their unimportance to those not vitally interested, were seized upon and passed from mouth to mouth. Hence it happened that Suzanna's departure that morning was known to all. The ostensible reason for her going had caused a murmur of approval among the peons of the two haciendas. They naturally wondered, now, what reason she had for being back. As is the way of men and women in their social position, they looked to their master for enlightenment, and the scowl which they saw upon Don Fernando's face, as well as the strained look in the eyes of Doña Luz, hinted that all was not well.

But as great as was Don Fernando's surprise upon beholding Suzanna, it did not match his son's.

Ramon blinked his eyes as he stared at her, believing they deceived him. What sort of miracle had happened to bring Suzanna here? As he continued to gaze at her spellbound, he saw her raise her eyes to him appealingly. The unfriendly attitude of those who confronted her had chilled the girl to her soul, and she turned to Ramon beseechingly.

"You?" Don Fernando thundered as his father glared at her. "What does this mean?"

Don Diego stepped out then, and threw his arms about his old friend.

"It means that I took mercy on her. It was worthy of you, old friend, to want to educate her, but as Suzanna asked me,—what can a peon do with an education?"

CHAPTER XIII

It cannot be said that Suzanna's return cast a shadow over the festivities Don Fernando and Doña Luz had arranged in honor of their neighbor. For, no matter what secret misgivings the girl's presence caused Señor Gutierrez and his wife, they had no desire to let Don Diego see how sorely Ramon's conduct tried them.

Even as short as was the distance between the two haciendas, Don Fernando felt that it offered some obstacle to a clandestine affair, and so he readily consented to having Suzanna become Chiquita's maid. This move was particularly galling to Ramon. If his father had deliberately tried to show him the gulf between Suzanna and himself, he could not have moved more surely. The boy felt that it was a slap at him, and he resented it bitterly.

Ramon's parents found Chiquita very beautiful; but Doña Luz viewed her imperious ways with

some alarm. She knew her son well enough to
know that arrogance would never win him. Don
Fernando was deaf to this criticism of his friend's
daughter. He could not close his eyes, however,
to the fact Chiquita had not swept his son off his
feet, for the boy made no effort to see her, but kept
to himself, sullen and untalkative.

Chiquita was well satisfied that he remained
away. Her surprise at finding Montesoro here in
California was concealed only by a supreme effort.
The man had left her without a word. That the
thought of seeing her again had brought him this
distance from the land he loved was a delicious
morsel for Chiquita. Best of all, she saw that her
father accepted him without suspicion. She had
expected to be bored to distraction, but instead she
found herself taking an eager interest in life.
Three days had elapsed since her return and
Pancho had not yet endeavored to see her. She
explained this to herself quite satisfactorily; but
the caution the man showed irked her.

She swept into her room one evening and caught
Suzanna admiring a modish gown of silk and lace.
Annoyed, Chiquita showed it by slamming the door
behind her.

Suzanna had gotten on better than she had supposed possible. Unaware that Pancho's continued absence had begun to fret her mistress, and that she had provoked her further, she blundered by saying naïvely:

"Life here must be very dull for you after all the gaieties of Mexico City."

Chiquita shot a shrewd glance at her. Her first thought being that she might have betrayed herself; but finding nothing in the girl's expression to alarm her, she smiled at the implied question.

The smile disarmed Suzanna, and she asked:

"Did you have many admirers?"

Chiquita was vain enough to answer honestly:

"Yes; quite a few."

She had seated herself before her mirror and was busy with her hair. Suzanna watched her with ill-concealed envy as she fingered her gold mounted toilette articles.

Ruiz, who had come on some errand, passed Chiquita's window at that instant, and catching sight of the beautiful girl, he stopped and gazed at her with adoring eyes. Chiquita banged the shutters in his face. Suzanna would have done well to have given up her attempt to engage her mistress in conversation, but she would pursue it.

"Didn't you like one of them very,—very much?" she asked.

Suzanna had unwittingly placed an emphasis on what Chiquita quickly interpreted to refer to her relation with Pancho. It angered her, and added to her indignation against Ruiz, caused her to reprimand Suzanna.

"You are entirely too familiar for a servant," she said tartly. "Your question is decidedly impudent. After this, you do your work and keep your tongue in your head."

Suzanna said nothing, but busied herself with putting away her mistress' gowns. That finished, she started to prepare her bed. The moon was up, and Chiquita had opened her shutters again and lounged indolently in a chair before the window.

A cooling breeze crept into the apartment as Suzanna finished her work. She was about to say good-night when from outside the bedroom window came the sound of a guitar.

Chiquita sat up as she recognized the tune. It was *Te Amo* (I love you). She had heard it many times, and she surmised the identity of the man who was strumming it now.

The melody was not unknown to Suzanna, and slipping up behind Chiquita, she endeavored to peek out. Her mistress saw her, however, and turned upon her angrily.

"Leave the room," she commanded. "Does your impudence know no restraint whatsoever?"

Suzanna bowed humbly and quitted the chamber; but her heart was heavy. Who else but Ramon would dare or have reason to serenade Chiquita de Sola?

Having rid herself of Suzanna, Chiquita stepped out upon the tiny balcony outside her window. With thudding heart she swept the patio for sight of the serenader.

"Here, dear one," a voice whispered.

"You, Pancho?" the girl gasped with a glad little cry as she saw Montesoro atop the patio wall. "Come nearer," she entreated.

The man slid along the wall until he was close enough to grasp the hand which Chiquita extended. He kissed it passionately.

"Ah, Pancho," the girl murmured, "how I have longed for you. How come you here?"

"Because of you," Montesoro answered. "No sooner had I learned that your father was returning with you than I made my plans. He does not recognize me. Don't be frightened. There is no danger."

"But there is," Chiquita warned, "if you are caught *here*. This is not Mexico City."

"You mean young Gutierrez?"

"He is nothing to me," the girl exclaimed. "It is my father who is to be feared. He talks of nothing else but my marriage. But oh, I am longing to be in your arms."

The man saw her breast heave with emotion as she leaned toward him.

"Then let me come in," he begged.

"That you cannot," Chiquita breathed in his ear. "It is too dangerous; besides, the gate is locked," she added compromisingly.

"I can manage it over the wall. Look into the patio from the other window. If it is deserted I am going to enter."

Chiquita hurried across the room, and after a careful examination of the garden tripped back to the man outside her window.

"We are alone," she murmured. "But do you think it is safe?"

Pancho nodded his head, and without further ado dropped into the enclosed garden.

Chiquita swayed upon her feet as she turned and caught up her mantilla. Throwing it over her shoulders, she crept downstairs and hurried into the patio. With a low cry, she threw herself into her lover's arms. They kissed then—for an eternity it seemed to little Suzanna who had stolen downstairs and hidden herself in a small store-room which gave onto the garden. She breathed a sigh of relief when the kiss ended,—glad that Chiquita's wooer was not Ramon; but horrified to find that the woman whom he was to take to wife should shame him so brazenly.

To add to Suzanna's excitement, Chiquita led Pancho to a bench which stood just outside the doorway of the store-room. Montesoro immediately launched into a long and detailed explanation regarding his presence in California. Suzanna heard enough to realize that he and Chiquita had carried on a very intimate affair in Mexico City.

"What is it that you intend to do?" she heard Don Diego's daughter ask.

"Marry you," Pancho replied.

"But you cannot," the girl protested. "I know

for a certainty my father will never give his consent."

"Then you must elope with me," Montesoro declared.

"But father surely would disinherit me," Chiquita replied. "And then where would we be? You have no money; neither have I."

"Very true," Pancho agreed. "But I am certain your father will readily forgive us when I convince him that I am worthy of your love and of the honor of being his son-in-law."

"Then why not convince him beforehand?" asked Chiquita.

"Because, as you say, he would never give his consent. He has set his heart upon your marrying Ramon, and will consider no other. But if you were to marry me, he would be soon reconciled, and readily give us his blessing."

"But what of Ramon?" queried the girl doubtfully.

"Ramon will marry you only over my dead body," Pancho declared fiercely.

Chiquita was about to capitulate when some one opened a door and stepped into the patio. It was her father. She saw him glance anxiously about the garden. Dreading that he would discover her, Chiquita took Montesoro's hand and led him into the store-room.

"We shall be safe here," she whispered. "Come, enfold me. I am dying of love for you."

Chiquita had her well-formed back toward Suzanna, but the very nearness of the girl and her lover was enough in itself to confound her. She wanted to escape, to get away from the scene being enacted before her, but she was helpless to do it. Even the shifting of the weight of her body from one foot to the other caught Montesoro's ear, for Suzanna saw him stiffen.

The eyes of the two lovers soon became accustomed to the darkness of the room. Chiquita lay in the man's arms, her sensuous eyes half-closed. Pancho, glancing over her shoulder, found himself staring at Suzanna.

He said nothing, but the girl in his arms felt his muscles tense, and sensing that something was amiss, she straightened.

Suzanna saw that she was discovered, and throwing caution to the winds made a bold attempt to reach the door. Montesoro intercepted her, and forcing her back into the room, he stepped through the door himself. Hot words were sure to follow between Chiquita and Suzanna, with the probability that Don Diego would overhear them and investigate. Pancho had no intention of ruining his chances by attempting to brazen out his *amour*. Unfortunately for him, he almost collided with Ruiz as he left the store-room. The old man had been searching for Suzanna, and the sight of Montesoro led him to the instant suspicion that he would find his daughter within the room the fellow had just quitted. Neither spoke in the brief instant that they faced each other. Pancho moved off then, maneuvering to bring the store-room between himself and Ruiz. This accomplished, he was about to vault to the top of the patio wall when he saw Don Diego again come to the door of the casa. Slipping back into the shadow, Pancho retraced his steps until he had gained the rear of the store-room.

Ruiz had opened the door in time to see Chiquita bring her hand down upon Suzanna's mouth.

"I'll teach you to spy on me, you impudent peon!" he heard her threaten.

Ruiz was not slow to gather that it had been Chiquita, and not Suzanna, who had been trysting with the man who had just left. The old servant was short-tempered as a rule, but rarely ever thoroughly angry. Hatred blazed in his eyes now as he beheld the lengths to which this girl went.

Chiquita had heard him enter, and she turned on him in a very froth of rage.

"Ruiz," she cried, "if you don't lash this spying daughter of yours, I shall see to it that the punishment is visited upon you. She is a loose-tongued, impertinent busy-body. San Luis Bautista was too good for her! But I can understand why your master wanted her sent away. Well, you remember this,—there are other places than the Mission to which peons can be sent."

Suzanna had not said a word; but her eyes conveyed every bit of the contempt which she felt for the woman before her. She looked to Ruiz for advice. He motioned for her to leave.

"Go to your room," he ordered. "And let no word of this affair pass your lips. I shall speak to you later."

Chiquita started to follow Suzanna, but Ruiz, transformed from the humble servant to a man of determination, stopped her.

"What is it you want?" Chiquita demanded almost insolently.

"A word with you," Ruiz replied with strange dignity.

The girl openly smiled her contempt for this old servitor. "Say your word quickly," she said sullenly.

"It is something that cannot be saıc quıckly," Ruiz answered grimly. "Nor will it be pleasant to listen to, but it must be said. You have proven to me to-night as no one else could have done, that you cannot make a silk purse from a sow's ear."

Chiquita gasped at the boldness of the man's words.

"Silence!" she cried. "Are you aware that you address the daughter of Don Diego de Sola? You are more impertinent than your miserable daughter. Out of my way now, and rest assured that my father shall be apprised of your conduct."

Aghast, Chiquita saw Ruiz stand his ground.

"I warned you that what I had to say would come as a shock," he declared. "You have had every opportunity that a girl can have. I am sorry that you have not profited thereby. Your actions to-night show how little store you set by the honorable name you bear and how little respect you have for the man to whom you are promised."

The enormity of the peon's offense to her dignity left Chiquita speechless. Eyes snapping, she saw Ruiz shake his head regretfully as he surveyed her.

"My child," Ruiz muttered, "there is no truer saying than that blood will tell. In spite of all the advantages and training you have had you remain as you were born,—all peon."

The blood left the girl's face as she heard him out. Something seemed to be strangling her as she fought for speech. Her hands flashed to her beautiful throat as a stifled scream broke from her lips.

"*Oh, Virgen santisima que pasa?*" she moaned at last. "Have you gone mad? What is it that you are trying to say?"

"That you are my daughter," Ruiz answered doggedly.

A mad laugh greeted this amazing statement. The girl's eyes showed that she thought Ruiz had gone insane.

"No," he said answering her, "I am not mad. You are *my* daughter, even as Suzanna is the daughter of Don Diego. The two of you were born on the same day. Suzanna's mother, Doña Fe, died in childbirth. We were but a few in California in those days. The families of Don Fernando and Don Diego shared the same roof. We were gathered about Doña Fe's bedside when she passed away. You had been born some two hours earlier. Doctor Ramos told Don Diego that he feared little Suzanna would follow her mother to the grave. I overheard him, and believing the child would live but an hour or two, I foolishly contrived to put you in Suzanna's crib and Suzanna into the arms of your sleeping mother. I have had eighteen years in which to regret it. I had hoped to give you an opportunity to rise to a position far removed from any that the child of a peon could aspire to. Before you left for Mexico City I had reasons enough to fear for your future. I took heart again when Don Fernando told me that Ramon and you were betrothed. My old dreams of you came back. I saw you, my own flesh and blood, the wealthiest and most powerful woman in the entire province. To make your way easy, I even agreed to have Suzanna sent away, for I had seen how fond she was of Ramon. And I knew that he took a great interest in her. And here, on the third night after your return, I find you engaged in a vile *amour* with a man who advertises his true worth to all who have eyes in their heads."

Consternation no longer gripped Chiquita as Ruiz finished. Unbelief, ridicule, amusement were written large across her face. This preposterous tale was not even worth denying.

"And you—do you believe that any one will take stock in your weird story?" she asked patronizingly.

"It will be easily proven," Ruiz answered without hesitation. "I do not ask or expect affection or consideration from you for myself. But Don Fernando has been a good master. And Don Diego has repaid my treachery with years of kind treatment. I will not see them shamed publicly. And no matter what it may cost me, I warn you that unless you change your ways I shall confess."

The dignity and assurance of the man bore weight with the girl, and as the horrible feeling that she had listened to the truth settled upon her, she flew into a wild rage. The fool, to talk of affection! With pleasure, she could have seen him drawn and quartered.

"If ever you so much as breathe a word of this to a living soul," she threatened vengefully, "I will kill you with my own hands. What do you think Don Diego would do if he knew how you had tricked him?"

"I am already an old man," Ruiz answered. "Death holds no fear for me. I have kept step with it so long that when it calls me I shall not hold back. And remember that it is me who threatens, not you. Go to your room, now, and take stock of yourself."

He attempted to open the door for her, but the girl would have none of his assistance. She flung herself out of the place, and with a hard, metallic laugh, crossed the patio.

The old man came out a second after her. Head bowed, he shuffled across the moonlit garden toward the rear of the house.

Ruiz had done that which he had been intent on for many years. And now that he had whispered his story to the ears of her who had profited most by his treachery, he found himself even more miserable than he had been, for fear was now added to his tortures. He wondered what his fate would be if Don Fernando discovered what he had done. Would he be sent to the hemp fields in Mexico to wear his old fingers off in the broiling suns of Yucatan? Death would be preferable to that.

Ruiz had been a good man on the hacienda. Few had worked harder. Would his master forget that? He made the sign of the cross and mumbled a prayer for mercy as he trudged to his room. He had little hope that what he had said to his daughter would make her change her ways. She was a wilful, headstrong girl. It is significant that what paternal affection the man had was given to Suzanna, and not to his own child, and whenever he succeeded in rising beyond worrying about himself, it was of her, and not of Chiquita, that he thought.

Pancho Montesoro waited until long after Ruiz' going before he moved from his cover in back of the store-room. The man had heard every word of what went on between the girl and her father. The effect of it left him cold, un-nerved. Not until he had scaled the wall and returned to his quarters in Don Fernando's house did he give vent to his emotions. It frightened him to think how close he had been to running off with the girl. Her secret would have come out, and he would have been left with a penniless peon on his hands.

The narrowness of his escape continued to haunt the man as he fought for sleep. And then, as he lay tossing in his bed, he saw his golden opportunity,—Suzanna. He alone, excepting Ruiz, knew the truth concerning her. What easier than to keep his head on his shoulders and let Ramon marry Chiquita? That left him a free hand with Suzanna. And so roseate did his immediate future become that he was soon fast asleep.

CHAPTER XIV

CHIQUITA lay awake the following morning waiting for Suzanna to serve her breakfast. Propped up in her massive bed, clothed in lingerie which was a mass of silk and lace, the girl was a beautiful picture, for all that she had not spent a particularly restful night and that she was in none too good humor. When her sleepy eyes caught sight of a hand protruding through the peep-hole in the door, she frowned. But the sight of a letter in the hand changed matters. Jumping quickly from bed, she hurried to the door and took the note.

She had just climbed back into bed when Suzanna —a far different Suzanna than she had ever seen before—returned with her breakfast of chocolate, *tortilla*, butter and molasses. Suzanna placed the tray on the bed in front of Chiquita, who stared at her disdainfully. Suzanna didn't mind: she had decided to treat her mistress with as silent contempt as she could command. Being anxious to get rid of her maid, so she could read her letter, Chiquita directed her to get fresh molasses. Without a word, Suzanna took the molasses pitcher and left the room. Chiquita opened her letter and found that it was from Pancho. As she read, her brow contracted, and a dark, foreboding look appeared in her eyes.

The letter said:

"I realize it would be a serious mistake for you to elope with me as we planned. Using your own words, your father might disinherit you; and I have nothing to offer but my great love. By all means marry Ramon. What will there be to prevent us from being the same to each other as we have been in the past? I love you too much to ask you to take the great risk of turning your father against you. Believe me, always yours.
"P————."

Chiquita trembled with anger. She was in such mental agitation that her body quivered. Marry Ramon! Indeed! Climbing quickly from her bed she began to dress.

No sooner was Suzanna back than she ordered her to tell Don Diego that she wished to see him at once in her apartment.

She was pacing impatiently up and down her room when Don Diego entered. She had had a few minutes in which to get control of herself, and her conduct showed that she was not without a certain finesse at chicanery.

Instead of letting loose a torrent of angry words, she went up to the man whom she had always addressed as father and placed her arm about his neck and kissed him.

Don Diego was delighted.

"What is it, little one?" he asked affectionately.

Chiquita mustered a tantalizing pout to her lips, and gazing at Don Diego from the corners of her eyes, she said in gentle, pensive tones:

"Father, must we remain here?"

"Do you find life so dull?" Don Diego asked sympathetically.

Chiquita nodded her head.

"I know that I shall wither and die if I have to remain here," she murmured plaintively.

"But you will soon become accustomed to this new order of life, my child. Before long you and Ramon will be getting married; you will find that that alone will bring many new interests to you. In the end, you will not trade California for Mexico City. My fortune is invested here, it is my home.

And I love this broad land. You will, too, when the glamour of city life wears off."

"But I shan't, father," Chiquita protested. "I shall never like it here. Please, father, won't—won't you let me return to Mexico City?"

Don Diego was astounded. He could not believe that he had heard aright.

"What?" he demanded. "You go back to Mexico City alone? Are you mad to suggest such a thing? Do you think that I would allow you, a girl of your age, to commit such folly?"

Don Diego's voice had risen as the enormity of Chiquita's request mounted before his eyes. The mask had fallen from the girl's face as his anger blazed forth.

"I am old enough to know what I want to do!" she retorted. "I will not remain here!"

"But you will!" Don Diego exclaimed. "And I warn you, do not humble me by communicating your desire to Ramon's family."

"Ramon?" Chiquita echoed contemptuously. "I have been here three days and he has not been in my company a second, save for meeting me at table."

"You forget," Don Diego protested in kindlier

tone, "that the boy is no dandy. But what skill he lacks on the guitar, he more than makes up in his ability to manage his father's hacienda. If I had a son of my own I would not ask to have him more worthy than Ramon."

"I question only his interest in me," Chiquita pursued. "If you ask, I hold as little attraction for him as he does for me. I have heard whispers enough since my return. Why was Don Fernando sending this girl Suzanna away? Surely, you do not believe this fiction about educating her?"

"You do not mean to say that you are jealous of little Suzanna, do you?" Don Diego asked. "You know the pet Don Fernando made of her. She and Ramon grew up together. It is only natural that the boy should have an interest in her. I hold it to his credit; but your tone implies something that I do not want to hear on my daughter's lips. Banish such evil thoughts, and rest assured that the boy's intentions are honorable. And remember, too, that it is well to be suspicious of those who are too well versed in love."

Chiquita turned away with a sarcastic smile, and as she did so, Suzanna came in with the announcement that Ramon was downstairs.

Don Diego bowed her out of the room. There was a smile of happiness on his face as he turned to Chiquita.

"See!" he grinned. "The boy is fond of you. He is like his father; he is not to be hurried. Put on your prettiest smile, little one, and you will see how he will reward you."

Ramon was going to Monterey for the day and Doña Luz was responsible for his being at Don Diego's home this early in the morning. The boy's mother had insisted that he offer to do whatever errands he could for Chiquita. It .was a gentlemanly thing to do, and one which he could not refuse, even though he resented placing himself in a position which seemed to give encouragement to his father's plans in regard to Chiquita.

Suzanna had lingered with Ramon as long as she had dared when he arrived, and once out of Chiquita's room, she promptly returned for another minute with him. Even though being near to him filled her with happiness, she was not able to conceal the fact from the boy that she was far from being the carefree girl she had been.

"You are unhappy here, aren't you, *mucha-*

chita?" Ramon said softly.   "There's no one to make excuses for you, now, is there?"

Suzanna shook her head as she looked away, afraid to meet his eyes.

"My father sold you as though you were a slave," the boy went on bitterly.   " 'Twere a million times better that you had gone to San Luis Bautista than to serve the woman you do.   She was ever a haughty, ill-tempered person, and it is easy to see she has not changed her ways."

"Hush," Suzanna begged.

"The injusice of it burns me," the boy persisted in saying.   "It makes me envy Pérez his freedom. If I had the courage I, too, would turn outlaw. But you mark it well—the day will come when these things will not be tolerated in California. I am a free-man, the son of a don, and yet I am ordered about even as you are. I have seen this day coming a long while since, and yet two weeks ago I was happy, satisfied to wait for others to act. I'm done with dreaming, now."

Ramon saw Suzanna tremble as she stiffled a sob. Reaching out, he placed his hands upon her shoulders and wheeled her around so that she faced him.

"Suzanna," he murmured, "I beg of you, don't despair. I trust I have been a dutiful son: it is my wish to remain one. But I shall not become a traitor to myself even for the love I bear my parents."

"Your words are very virtuous," interrupted Chiquita. She had entered the room in time to catch Ramon's last statement and to see the tender regard for Suzanna in his eyes.

Ramon faced her rather truculently, feeling that she had contrived to steal into the room. Chiquita read the look in his eyes and deliberately set out to exasperate him by asking:

"Did you come to see me, or my maid?"

The boy did not answer at once. Instead he sur-surveyed her coldly. Then:

"Maids are so new a luxury in California that I recognize one with difficulty, especially when I am in the presence of two persons, one of whom I am pledged to wed, and the other, my playmate since childhood."

The reprimand in his words forced a grudgingly given nod of apology from Chiquita. This clash of wills opened her eyes to the mettle of the man. Not quite sure of herself, she heard Ramon say:

"As for the statement which you overheard, I can but say again that it is the truth. But I do beg you not to misinterpret my interest in this girl. My regard for her is honorable."

"And evidently most intimate," Chiquita added with biting sarcasm.

"Happily, yes," Ramon answered boldly.

"Then why do you announce yourself to me?"

"I am going to Monterey for the day. My mother thought that you might have need of something from the city."

"Your mother is most kind," Chiquita said condescendingly. "Please convey my thanks to her. My needs, though, are better served by one who deems it an honor, and not a duty, to administer to them."

Ramon took his dismissal gracefully. Chiquita bade Suzanna to open the door for him, but the boy sprang ahead of her, and bowing courteously, threw the door open and passed out. The next minute they heard him riding away.

Chiquita, unable to control herself longer, raised her clenched hands to her breasts as she confronted Suzanna.

"Go, you devil's whelp!" she stormed wrathfully. "Do not let me see your hateful face again this day. And if I ever find you in that man's company you shall be publicly flogged."

Suzanna was more than glad to do as she was ordered, and as she left the room she murmured to herself:

"O, Holy Mother, if this be a lady, then I am glad that I am a peon."

Her thought but echoed Ramon's. The impression of his bride-to-be which the boy had carried away with him was little calculated to make him look on her with less antipathy. From childhood, he had ever found Chiquita cold, haughty, and domineering. The traits which she had given evidence of possessing as a girl were in full bloom now, and Ramon's spirit revolted at the thought of giving the best years of his life to her.

"*I* am the chattel, not the peon," he mused as he raced his horse toward Monterey. "By what right of God or man does my father compel me to marry this woman? She has the shrewish temper of a crone, even though she is held up to me for an aristocrat. I'll have none of her; I am a free man, and I swear that my self respect shall not be taken from me. 'My maid,' " he quoted contemptuously. "Truth were better served if their positions were reversed."

CHAPTER XV

ALVAREZ HAS A VISITOR

ALVAREZ, the attorney, made a habit of arising with the sun. That very morning he had been wandering about the dew-laden patio of his modest home when his *mozo* brought him word of a visitor. The earliness of the hour prompted the thought that this client came on urgent business. He gave a thought to his person, and although he wore only a *serape* which barely came to his knees, leaving his bony shanks exposed, he decided to see his visitor at once. Ordering his servant to show the man into the patio, Alvarez paced back and forth nervously. He was a tall, angular man, fairly bald, and his present attire only served to make him more grotesque than usual. His surprise, when Ruiz was shown in, can be imagined.

"What brings you here at this hour of the day?" he demanded anxiously.

The peon's eyes were bloodshot; his thin face more wrinkled than ever. He had come the distance from the hacienda since midnight. His body quivered nervously, his hands clenching and unclenching as he stood before the lawyer.

Ruiz had tortured himself for hours with the thought that his secret was out at last. He cursed the impulse which had led him to tell Chiquita the truth. What if she should unwittingly betray him to Don Diego? His life would be forfeited without doubt. If she kept his secret, she would have him done away with to protect herself. His conduct had been unforgivable. In fancy, he saw every man's hand raised against him.

Ruiz was singularly human in his worry. As old age had crept on him he had become obsessed with the desire to tell his secret to some one. But now that he had, he would have sold his soul to have been able to recall his words. Worst of all for him, the conviction that he would have to confide in one of his betters and seek advice, had grown on him. He could not turn to Don Fernando or Don Diego, and so Alvarez, the lawyer, had seemed the next best friend. The desire to tell another, once acknowledged, Ruiz found himself done with sleep, and pursued by devils of his own conjuring, he had set off in the middle of the night for Monterey.

"I am in great trouble, Señor Alvarez," he muttered miserably in answer to the lawyer's question.

"You, Ruiz?" Alvarez exclaimed, surprised that the man came about his own affairs, and not Don Fernando's. The lawyer immediately dismissed from his mind the thought that anything serious impended. "I am sorry to hear you say so, Ruiz," he continued in lighter vein. "But what would happen to me if people did not encounter trouble once in a while? Come into the house and tell me your woes."

Only after considerable hemming and hawing did Señor Alvarez succeed in drawing the man's story from him. The attorney's shrewd eyes showed, as Ruiz continued, that he had reversed his opinion about this affair being a matter of no importance. By the time the peon had finished, he was keenly alive to his opportunity. And had Ruiz had a proper knowledge of men he would have seen the cunning in the lawyer's eyes as Alvarez spread his hands and said:

"This is a very, very serious matter, Ruiz. It involves my dearest friends. With all my legal knowledge, I am still constrained to say that there is nothing in law to right this wrong. The deception of a lifetime is not undone so easily. Don Diego is a hot, tempestuous gentleman. I do not doubt that your life would be in danger if he heard a word of what you have told me. Your master would be hardly less severe, for he has set his mind on Ramon's marrying Chiquita."

"What am I to do?" Ruiz groaned aloud.

"Keep your tongue in your head! Let no man know a word of this. I will give the matter my earnest attention, and when I have arrived at a solution I will notify you. It is a terrible thing to conceal, and may Heaven forgive me for advising you to seal your lips. But many times these matters work out their own solution. I want you to promise me, though, come what may, that you will never reveal the fact that you have consulted me."

Ruiz made the sign of the cross as he sank to his knees and pressed the lawyer's hand to his lips.

"Oh, Señor Alvarez," he promised, "I shall do as you say. I am only a poor, ignorant man; you have the wisdom of the world at your finger tips. I should have come to you months ago."

"Well, see that you return to the hacienda with

some speed or else Don Fernando will wonder what strange business has brought you to town. Be careful of whom you meet. I will be at the hacienda for the *fiesta*. If I have anything to communicate to you, I shall do so then."

But Ruiz had no sooner passed through the patio gate than the attorney dropped his mournful pose and rushing into the room where his son, Miguel, slept, he cried:

"Awaken! Arise at once!"

Miguel groaned, muttered an inarticulate word, and then turned over to woo sleep again.

His father caught him by the arm and half-pulled him out of his bed. The boy opened his blurred eyes in astonishment in answer to this violent treatment.

"What is it?—what is the matter?" he gasped.

"Matter enough," Alvarez retorted. "I want you to dress at once, and as soon as you have had your coffee, take yourself to Don Diego's hacienda. There is legal work awaiting me there which you can manage. Let that be your excuse. My real reason for sending you is that I want you where you can pay every attention to little Suzanna."

"Suzanna?" Miguel questioned in surprise.

"It is my wish that you marry her as speedily as you can manage it."

"You, my father, advise me to marry a peon?"

"Do not be troubled about that. She is a remarkable girl. I want you to move swiftly, and as you regard your well-being—with success. You can trust me for being no fool. Ask no questions; but do as I command."

The hazing which he had received at Suzanna's hands had not inspired Miguel with any desire to wed her. He shivered to think how she would receive his love-making. And although he feared his father, the boy stood in greater dread of Suzanna's sharp tongue.

"But I have no desire to wed Suzanna," he cried.

"Your desires are not to be considered," his father answered sharply. "I warn you—do not come running back to me with the word that she will have none of you. I know the girl; she is of a fine temper and a sharp tongue. If you fail to win her I shall disinherit you if it is the last act of my life."

Dumbfounded, the boy set about preparing for the journey. He knew his father to be a stern, severe man; what he did, he did cautiously, and

usually with wisdom. But what was there of caution or wisdom in this mad move? And Suzanna?
—thought of her made the boy move even more reluctantly. Didn't his father know that she would
laugh him to scorn if he attempted to woo her?
Only the sound of his father returning to see how
he got on made the boy hasten.

A half-hour later, his guitar thrown over his
shoulder, Miguel set forth for the hacienda. But
if ever a sadder or more hopeless knight set forth
in quest of fair lady, history does not record it.

CHAPTER XVI

CROSS PURPOSES

CHIQUITA lost little time in dispatching a note
to Montesoro, once Ramon had left. The customs
of the country allowed her liberties she never would
have known in a more urban atmosphere. Her
note to Pancho requested him to accompany her
on horseback that afternoon.

Pancho had greeted the new day with mind quite
made up as to his future conduct. The note from
Chiquita came as no great surprise. He resolved
to take advantage of the opportunity the ride would
afford, and come to a definite break with her. He
was early in keeping his appointment; this by design, too. He had hoped to find chance for a word
with Suzanna, and in this he was not disappointed.

"Your memory is very poor, señor," Suzanna
answered caustically to his compliments.

"But my eyes are not," Pancho grinned. "They
see that thou art as beautiful as ever."

" 'Twere best you saved your word for her

whose company you so enjoyed last night," Suzanna retorted.

"Thou art not jealous?" Pancho said teasingly.

"Humph!" The exclamation was bitterly sarcastic. "Your words but flatter yourself."

Pancho was not deterred from trying to make his point with her.

"A gentleman often does what is expected of him,—because it is expected." He dropped his voice and put a serious note into it as he proceeded.

"Let it remain for me to despise myself as I should," he muttered. "Only last night did I realize to what low station I had fallen to find happiness in an affair with one who by her conduct should be hailed as peon, not lady. This afternoon will see an end to it! I had hoped to win her father's patronage; but the need for that is gone. I have been in communication with certain gentlemen in Monterey, who are anxious to establish the sport of kings in their city. Arrangements are going forward for the building of an arena. In a few weeks I will be hailed as an idol in this province. But I shall not forget you, little one. I promise you, that as I live, I shall ask you to be my wife."

He had heard Chiquita leave the house, and without seeming to be aware of it, he turned from Suzanna without a further word, his face tense with well-feigned emotion.

Suzanna could but gaze after him dumbly. Truly, this was a new Pancho. She saw him bow coldly to her mistress, and offer what seemed to be a reluctant hand as he helped her into her saddle. The man's manner toward Chiquita was in marked contrast to the passionate fondness which he had shown the night before.

Not until a turn of the road hid them from view did Suzanna return to her work. Whatever relief she felt at having her mistress away for the afternoon was short-lived for she had barely composed herself when her eyes widened at the sight of Miguel Alvarez in holiday attire.

Suzanna greeted him with a laugh, but her face lost its smile as she began to realize that he came to pay her compliments. Miguel's efforts were clumsy to the point of being ridiculous.

"What is it you are trying to do?" Suzanna snapped as the fool boy persisted in annoying her with his declarations.

"I have come to marry you," Miguel answered sadly.

"You have, eh?" Suzanna showed her teeth in a mirthless grin. What had happened to the world? Here was the second man within the hour who had proposed to her. Suzanna shook her head as she studied the boy's face. "Even the thought of it seems to make you miserable," she said sharply. "You know as little of women as you do of game-cocks! Holy Mother of God!——what madman whispered to you that I could care for you? Tell me, why should I want to wed you?"

"I have an honorable name," Miguel retorted, stung to the quick by Suzanna's derision. "I have my father's permission to wed you, too. I am an only son. Some day I shall have means. Do you think to do better than wed one of my station As my wife, you will be received with the courtesy your beauty deserves."

"You think, then, to exhibit me as though I were a prize bull, eh? I'll have none of it! Peon I am, though you do not put it into words; but even so, I shall wed a man, and not a monk."

"Well I know on whom your heart is set," Miguel argued more bravely than he felt. "But

you will never get him. I do not ask you for love;
but you shall wed me."

"Shall?" Suzanna mocked. " 'Tis a strong
word."

"No stronger than my purpose, I swear. I have
work here at the hacienda which will occupy me
some days. I assure you I will not leave until the
two purposes of my visit have been accomplished."

"You bluster as though you were in a court-
room," Suzanna exclaimed. "Small thought have
I for what brings you here. Take off with your
ranting, or I shall cry out to the first one who
passes."

Unconsciously, Suzanna had raised her voice
until it had attracted the attention of Don Diego
who sat in his study. Coming to the door, he saw
Alvarez' son, and, surmising that the loud talking
which he had heard had been occasioned by the
boy's arrival, led him into the house without further
questioning.

If the last half-hour had been unpleasant for
Suzanna, it had been none the less so for Chiquita.
She and Pancho had not more than passed from
sight of the house before she said:

"I received your letter this morning."

Pancho had glanced at her keenly, but her face was turned from him, and he could not determine her expression. Her voice, however, was casual enough. He replied:

"Beautiful one, it grieved me more than I can express to write that letter; but I love you too much to take you away from the luxurious life to which you have been accustomed."

This concern for her did not aid in restoring Chiquita's good humor.

"But you said at one time that my father would certainly accept you as a son-in-law after we were married," she argued.

"Yes, I know," Pancho agreed, "but that was before I knew how deeply your father had set his heart upon your marrying Ramon."

"But I have no intention of marrying Ramon," the girl declared.

"But you must, my sweetheart," Montesoro urged. "It is your father's wish, and you must abide by it. Regardless of the great love I bear for you, and you for me, marriage between us is impossible. Your father would surely disinherit you, and as I have nothing more to offer than my love, your loss would be too great."

Pancho was exerting himself to the utmost to be convincing, but there was a false note in his voice which did not entirely escape Chiquita.

"Why do you speak for Ramon?" she asked suspiciously. "What has brought about this sudden change in your feeling for me?"

"Do you doubt my love?" Pancho demanded angrily.

"Oh, no—no," Chiquita hastened to reply. "Only——"

"Well then, there is no reason why we cannot be friends even though you are Gutierrez' wife," Montesoro went on ruthlessly. "And remember,— some husbands do not live long."

Chiquita shot a startled glance at the man as she saw him pat his sword meaningly. This willingness to do murder did not satisfy her. She wanted love, not violence. Woman-like, she sensed the gulf which had opened between them, and it was her intention to bridge it at once.

"But how can I marry a man whom I despise?" she insisted.

"It is your father's doing, not mine," Montesoro protested. "Had I the least to offer you, I should laugh at his wishes. Alas that I am impoverished to the point where I am forced to linger beneath a roof where I am no longer welcome. They have guessed my interest in you. I shall take my leave soon. This morning I posted word to Monterey agreeing to appear in the bull-ring this fall."

Chiquita's face blanched at this.

"You mean that you are going to flaunt your profession in my father's face? Then, indeed, will he be done with you."

"A man must live; and there are those who hold it no disgrace to claim a *torero* for son-in-law."

This flat declaration carried a world of meaning to the girl. She became obsessed with the fear that she had lost the man forever. For the first time, Montesoro found tears in her eyes; and if there had been one thing necessary to turn him completely against her, this was it. Chiquita was not without cleverness, and she realized too late that she played a losing hand.

The ride was cut short as a consequence, and an hour later they returned to the house. Neither spoke as they rode into the patio. Montesoro caught sight of Suzanna sitting upon the balcony outside Chiquita's window. He knew he was being watched. Hardly a second later, Chiquita saw the girl, and her bad humor increased accordingly.

"She's a fascinating little thing," Pancho muttered to his companion as he helped her down. "You had better lose no time with Ramon," he warned.

The effect of this was to send the girl into a violent rage, and had not Don Diego and Miguel came toward them, Montesoro would have paid the penalty for his words.

Señor de Sola greeted the man cordially and smiled on his daughter. "Already one arrives for the *fiesta*," he said happily. "Miguel brings you a gift from his father and himself."

"You should be very happy, Don Diego," Pancho observed before Chiquita could frame a reply. "I was just congratulating your daughter on the very pleasant future which lies before her as the wife of Don Ramon."

Although she could have killed the man for his impudence, Chiquita bravely managed a smile as Don Diego took her into his arms and kissed her. Almost for the first time did she stop to contemplate the magnitude of the debt which she owed him. It left her weak, impotent in her anger.

Fear swooped down upon her as she entered the house. She was afraid to ask herself what her fate would be should this man, who had done so much for love of her, learn the truth.

Don Diego little guessed the agony which possessed the girl. Nor did she see the mist which swam in his eyes as she impulsively threw her arms about his neck and pulled down his head to whisper into his ear:

"Father,—do not let us delay the day."

CHAPTER XVII

THE PRICE OF FEAR

MIGUEL did his best to make the most of the opportunities his stay at the hacienda afforded him; but the day of the *fiesta* arrived without his having succeeded in turning Suzanna's wrath. The boy dreaded to see his father come. From experience, he knew that excuses carried little weight with him. And although Miguel was not the only one on the two haciendas whose heart was sorely tried, it is true that he alone failed to respond to the excitement of the day.

Don Diego had spared no expense in the preparations for the *fiesta*. Ladies and gentlemen came from as far away as Monterey to wish him well. Steers had been slaughtered and prepared for the barbecue; vegetables and fruits gathered; wines brought forth and tested; flowers plucked and woven into garlands to decorate pillars and tables.

At sun-up many quarters of beef has been placed upon the spits to roast; steer heads, properly wrapped to insure that appetizing flavor which only barbecued meat possesses, buried among the glowing coals; while in the outdoor ovens *tortillas* in squadrons began to brown.

As the morning advanced, the guests came in greater numbers until noon-time found more than a hundred merrymakers gathered on the hacienda. Don Diego's servants moved among them with food and drink. Small attention was paid to the wants of the inner man at this time. The feasting would come after an afternoon of games; of feats of strength for the young men; of horsemanship for the skilled riders; and of gambling, true to relate, for older heads. The crowd was anxious to be at its play, and sounds of laughter and excitement filled the patio and compound.

Suzanna had not been able to resist the spirit of the occasion. She had attended many similar *fiestas* at the surrounding ranchos, and her acquaintances were many. Once free of her duties, she mingled with the throng and soon her merry laughter drove the frowns from her face.

Ramon happened to catch sight of her, and he grinned to himself at seeing her so happy again.

For the first time in days he found her the Suzanna of old.

Señor Alvarez had scolded his son most roundly for having failed to make progress with the girl. He promptly ordered Miguel to make haste and take advantage of this day which was to order for swains. Miguel had not dared to dissent. Suzanna had shaken him off several times already, and as Ramon watched, he saw the boy approach her again. This time, Suzanna boxed his ears and called down upon him the laughter of the crowd. Ridicule, heaped on in such generous portioning, was more than Miguel could stand, and father or not, he beat his retreat.

Ramon smiled at the boy's chagrin, although he half-suspected that Miguel had serious designs on Suzanna, so persistent had he been these last days. But Miguel was not of a cut to arouse jealousy in the breast of a lover.

One other, Montesoro, grinned, too; but more from a sense of relief than from pleasure. He had found Miguel in his way wherever he chanced on Suzanna, and he had accepted him as a rival, even though an awkward one. Pancho was wise enough to take a leaf from Miguel's book, and accordingly, he left Suzanna to her own devices.

Arm in arm with his loyal friend, Don Fernando, Don Diego walked among his guests with a warm word for each. The upset condition of the province was forgotten. Here was plenty for all; and no man so mean but he was welcome. Even a dusty friar traveling Montereyward by foot was urged to tarry, and offered food and wine.

Upon the wide portico of the large house Doña Luz and Chiquita mingled with other ladies of high estate. Ramon's mother found the girl unduly thoughtful of her.

Chiquita was most anxious to appear at her best. The fear that her secret would find her out had been fanned by misgivings of one sort or another until her heart missed a beat every time some one spoke suddenly to her.

Long before the sounding of a gong announced that the feast was ready, savory odors from the pits had whetted the appetites of the merrymakers. Eagerly, then, they gathered around the festive board and toasted their host with a rare wine of his own vintage.

Don Diego was a proud and happy man as he

faced his guests,—Chiquita at his left, Doña Luz at his right. The girl's excitement had sent a high color to her cheeks and she was radiant. Don Diego glanced at her approvingly as the meal progressed, unaware of the unhappiness which clutched her.

A platform had been built for dancing, and now the musicians appeared and launched forth on the *jota*. Almost immediately a young couple ran to the platform and began dancing. When they had finished, another couple re-placed them; then another and another.

Finally the music changed, and now poured forth a sharper melody. Suddenly Suzanna darted from the edge of the crowd to the dancing floor.

Sprightly, agile,—as light on her feet as the gentle summer's-evening breeze—Suzanna floated over the ground, her lithe body swaying from side to side, her slender legs flashing now and again from within the be-ruffled skirts that encompassed them. Around and around glided the girl, her eyes sparkling, her lips half-apart, her body rhythmically swaying from side to side.

From within the crowd came a hat, tossed by a hopeful *caballero*—hopeful that Suzanna would accept him for her partner. But Suzanna kicked the hat aside disdainfully. Instantly it was replaced by another, and still another. Each was accorded the same treatment. Pancho's beautiful sombrero found its way to a point in front of Suzanna. With even more disdain than she had accorded the others, she kicked it aside.

Ramon had watched Suzanna dance with a smile on his lips. When Suzanna had disdained Pancho's challenge, he grinned happily, arose from his seat beside Chiquita, removed his sword and its scabbard, and picking up his sombrero, tossed it toward Suzanna. She recognized it, and without stopping, circled around and about it, swaying and gliding with all the abandon of a healthy young animal. Then, for an instant, she paused, and deliberately jumped upon Ramon's hat. She had accepted his challenge!

Without more ado, Ramon left Chiquita's side, and joined Suzanna. There before the gathered multitude they stood,—hands raised above their heads, gazing into each other's eyes.

The music resumed, and the crowd held its breath, for though Suzanna had danced with surpassing grace alone, she outdid herself now. Apparently each had forgotten those gathered about them. Poetry was in every motion of their bodies. Alert, eyes flashing, the intoxicating music carried them on and on until they seemed to be drawn out of themselves, holding each other by the spell of their eyes alone.

It was interpretive dancing without being intended as such. Pancho read its story; but not less clearly than did Chiquita. Intuition told her that these two loved each other as few men and women do. It was in every step they took. Were these others blind that they did not see it?

The girl's hatred of Suzanna overwhelmed her as she watched. Horrified, she asked herself if this was but like finding like. For all of her low position, did Ramon find, sub-consciously, in Suzanna, the lady, and in herself, the peon?

She would have laughed had any one told her she could be jealous of Ramon; and yet jealousy gripped her now. Pancho's lightly turned warning came back to her. What would she do if Ramon took it into his head to run away with Suzanna? The thought threw her into a panic. Without considering the consequences of her act, she grasped the arm of Don Diego, who had been watching the dancers, an indulgent smile on his face.

"Father," she murmured brokenly, "It is my wish that you announce my bethrothal publicly to-night."

Don Diego's happiness engulfed him. Tears came to his eyes as he pressed the girl to him.

"What a wonderful moment," he murmured. "You make this a real *fiesta* for me. Mother Church shall publish the bans at once."

Don Fernando and Doña Luz greeted the good news with evident happiness.

"And shall we set a day for the wedding?" Don Fernando asked eagerly.

Chiquita bowed her head in assent. "It will please me to marry your son as soon as the Church permits."

Don Fernando kissed her fatherly. "It can be arranged," he announced. "We have waited over-long already. Is a week from to-day too soon?"

"It is quite agreeable to me," Chiquita answered humbly. "My father presented me with a most wonderful trousseau before we left Mexico City."

"Then it is arranged!" exclaimed Don Diego,

a broad smile on his face. "The other matters can be attended to in time."

Don Fernando's eyes swept the room in search of his son. Ramon and Suzanna had just finished their dance, and the girl was seated upon his knee now, out of breath.

The crowd made way for Don Fernando who, without considering Suzanna, took Ramon by the arm and led him toward the table where Chiquita, Don Diego and Doña Luz were waiting. The crowd, sensing something out of the ordinary, closed in behind them. And poor Suzanna, startled out of a year's growth, was left alone in the center of the floor, trying to imagine what the trouble might be. She was not long in doubt, for above the murmuring of the crowd, Don Diego's soft voice arose portentously.

"My friends," he said, "this is one of the happiest moments of my life. I take infinite pleasure in informing you that my daughter Chiquita wishes her betrothal to Don Ramon, son of my beloved friend, Don Fernando, announced this night. And further, that the wedding shall take place one week from this day. Will you drink with me, my friends, to their unending happiness?"

A great cry arose as this startling news swept over the room. Goblets were held aloft and their contents drained with avidity. Ladies and gentlemen, peons, unlettered Indians,—all crowded about the betrothed couple and their parents, showering them with congratulations and good-will.

Dumbly, Ramon heard himself addressed and complimented. His mumbled replies were unintelligible to both his friends and himself. The suddenness with which he had been plunged to the depths left him helpless. With eyes hard, his lips compressed as his teeth sank into them, he sent an appealing glance toward the spot where he had left Suzanna. But Suzanna did not catch the look, for fainting, she had sank to her knees; and as Ramon stared, he saw Pancho lift her to her feet and lead her out into the patio.

Chiquita caught the look on Ramon's face, and felt well repaid for what her decision cost her.

Montesoro's interest in Suzanna, however, did not rest so well with her. Her keen eyes had seen how tenderly he had lifted the girl to her feet. The protecting arm which he had placed about her as he led her from the room hinted at more than the courtesy of a gentleman to one who was socially his inferior. A tragic thought swept through Chiquita's brain as she considered this. Was it possible that the man was in love with that peon? Had she bewitched him as she had Ramon? Could it be possible that Pancho had spurned her so that he could advance his position with her maid?

The thought continued to grow on her as she faced it, and she was more than pleased when Don Diego, who having noticed her nervousness, suggested that she excuse herself to her guests. Alone in her room, Chiquita's emotion overcame her, but she consoled herself with one thought. Come what may, she had Ramon.

CHAPTER XVIII

"THE WORLD'S A STAGE."

SUZANNA'S heart was breaking as Montesoro led her to a bench in the moonlit garden and sat down beside her. And though her lips quivered, strange as it may seem, her eyes were dry. Don Diego's announcement had sounded the knell of dreams which she had not known were her life's blood.

Pancho knew what she was passing through, and as immeasurable as his ego was, he rose above it now and consoled her as best he could. Fate played into his hands this once, for inasmuch as he was the only one who seemed to care what happened to her, Suzanna warmed to him as most human beings would have done in the same circumstance.

For the first time, Montesoro saw that his tenderness toward her was not repulsed. With rare wisdom he kept from trying to advance his own cause by word of mouth; and not until Suzanna had found relief in tears did he try to influence her.

"But surely you had been warned that this was to happen," he murmured softly. "That it came to-night, Suzanna, was largely your fault."

"My—my—fault?" Suzanna asked between sobs.

"Yes. I guessed it some time before Don Diego spoke. Chiquita's eyes never left you as you danced with Ramon. She saw the truth in a flash. If ever jealousy swept a woman off her feet it did to-night. I know her better than you suppose. She's got the temper of a fiend."

"Well I know it," Suzanna answered, staring off into space.

"Do you think that I would have come all the way from Mexico City to be near her if I had known that she was betrothed to another man? Even though I am not the son of a blueblood, I bow my head to none. She but played with me at first, and I knew it. I swore to myself that I would humble her, and I did. She begged me,—actually begged me to run away with her."

Pancho's speech grew so vehement that Suzanna looked at him rather fearfully.

"Maybe you can understand, now, why she hates and despises me," he went on. "She was ripe for

what happened to-night. She knew she had lost
me, and I could see her asking herself if you, a
peon, were to steal this other man away from her.
She thinks to hurt me, too.”

Pancho laughed at the impossibility of it.

“When she learns that it is you whom I really
love she will die of hatred.”

“Oh, hush,” Suzanna begged as he reached for
her hand. “Please don’t.”

“It’s the truth, and you know it. Surely, Suzanna, you did not expect Ramon to renounce the
empire which will be his when his father dies, or
to disregard the fact that you are of peon stock.
No! In the short time that I have been here I have
seen that Don Fernando sets more store by his
lineage than he does by his wealth. The boy has
been brought up to believe the same. He is only
a human being, Suzanna,—you ask too much of
him.”

The man but echoed her own thoughts, so
Suzanna could do naught but nod her head af-
firmatively.

“Don’t think that Ramon does not care for you,”
he declared with fervor. “He does! The asso-
ciations of childhood, the many happy hours you

spent together,—he is not deaf to them. But" and Pancho shook his head sadly, "it is not the affection a man has for a woman without whom life is impossible. If what I say is not true, do you think he would have left you alone to-night without a word? When a man loves, as I love you, he would do anything to win the heart of her whom he adores,—and not count the cost, either."

Suzanna glanced at him beseechingly.

"Please," she entreated, "Do not talk of love to me to-night. My heart is far too heavy to listen."

"Forgive me," Pancho begged. "My own heart breaks to see you so unhappy. I want to take you into my arms and caress you and drive your tears away. But here I sit, helpless before you."

And because she was so distraught and because the man revealed himself so different from what he had been, Suzanna gave him her hand. The man's eagerness almost overcame him. He but pressed it tenderly.

"You have seen me at my worst," he said haltingly as he got to his feet. "I am done with idling. My one thought from now on is to make myself worthy of you, for come what may I shall make you my wife, Suzanna. And now, if you are composed, we will go back to the others."

"Leave me alone here, please, for a few minutes," Suzanna replied. "I want to be by myself for a moment or two."

Pancho bowed, and with a fervent word, went back to the house. The man had reason to congratulate himself. He had not made a single mis-step.

CHAPTER XIX

"I WOULD SERVE YOU WELL."

Now, it so happened that the poor friar, who had been invited to join the guests of Don Diego, had partaken too often of his host's rare wines, and in consequence, he had sought refuge in a shady bower within the patio some time since. For one who was supposed to have succumbed to the sprites which lurk in the flowing bowl, he had taken a very keen interest in what went on between Suzanna and Montesoro. The stillness of the garden made it no great task to overhear what had been said. He sat now with a puzzled frown upon his broad features. The man was plainly nettled, and most certainly not the worse for liquor. He was seated so that he could study the girl as she sat by herself, lost in her thoughts. It was while engaged in this pleasant occupation that Alvarez and Miguel came into the patio. They entered by a side door which led them onto a path that wound by the bower in which the humble padre sat.

The friar closed his eyes and resumed his snoring as the two approached him. Señor Alvarez was speaking as Miguel caught sight of the man and cautioned his father accordingly.

" 'Tis but a drunken friar, who half-starved from his infernal fasting has fallen an easy prey to Don Diego's cellar," Alvarez assured his son. "Come, find Suzanna. She is alone here somewhere. There,—do you see her?" Alvarez looked at Miguel for an answering nod. "Well, remember she is in a mood for kind words. Do not scold her for daring to raise her eyes to Ramon. Use diplomacy,—be affable, remind her that she would do well to accept your name."

Alvarez paused, and then in a voice which carried its own threat he warned:

"Do not forget what I said to you in Monterey. You *must* win her. If you fail to make her your wife I shall cut you off without a cent. Some boys with half your prospects would lead her to the altar in less time that it takes to tell it. Do not come back to me with more excuses."

Miguel had no protest to make. He had long since exhausted argument. For some unknown reason his father had doomed him to the fate ahead of him, and he was powerless to do aught but proceed as he was ordered.

The snoring friar sat erect immediately that he was alone. First making sure that Alvarez had actually returned to the house, he sat himself to watch the movements of Miguel.

Suzanna, weary in body and soul, greeted the boy as though he were another torture which she had to bear. Miguel began his protestations at once, and the girl, too weary to stop him, permitted him to run on without interruption.

What he said was lost on Suzanna. She was aware of it only as one is conscious of the droning of a bee. The boy began to realize as much, and he stopped short.

"Won't you even answer me?" he demanded humbly.

"Yes, go!" Suzanna snapped. "Get out! Leave me alone! I am wearied to death with your chattering."

"But my father," Miguel protested. "I have got to marry you. He demands it."

"What,—your father?" demanded Suzanna, showing interest for the first time in the boy's words. "What fool's talk is this? Why should your father insist that you marry me?"

"I do not know," the unhappy Miguel replied. "He sent me here."

"Well, I'll send you back to him! And tell him that I would not marry you if you were the last man in the world. Tell him that I am promised to another," Suzanna lied as she sent the boy away. "Tell him anything you please; but this for you,— if you come near me again I shall let Timoteo claw your eyes out."

The friar sat where he was for some time after Miguel had gone. Tears were stealing down Suzanna's cheeks, and when the sound of her crying reached him, he got up, and after pulling his hood low over his head, walked toward her.

Suzanna heard the pebbles crunching under his feet as he approached, and she looked up at him as he stopped in front of her.

"Child," he said kindly, "you seem most unhappy, and that too amidst scenes of great gayety. Allow me to solace you."

Without further ado he took the seat Miguel had so recently quitted, and turning toward Suzanna found her staring at him curiously.

“Your voice is strangely familiar, good padre,” she exclaimed. “By what name are you called?”

“Lores,—Padre Lores, my child,” the friar replied. “From yonder bower I have seen you dismiss two young men within the last half hour; both of whom seemed most intent on winning your favor. And yet from experience with youth do I know that only a young man can be the excuse for the tears which I see in your eyes. Tell me, what manner of man can he be to seek for fairer face than yours?”

The friar had taken Suzanna’s hand within his own, and he petted it gently as he waited for her to reply. The man’s presence seemed to give her comfort, and without knowing why, she found herself anxious to talk to him.

“He is a noble gentleman, Padre Lores,” Suzanna murmured wistfully. “I—as you see from my clothes—am a peon. I have wrought my own unhappiness. I should have known that the liberties allowed me in childhood were only indulgences to a child; that the barrier against my class would be raised as I approached womanhood.”

“You almost tell me the gentleman’s name. For what should send you away from the gay throng inside but the announcement of the betrothal?”

The friar was silent for a moment, looking off at the distant hills outlined by the rising moon. Suzanna thought she felt a tremor pass through his body.

“And you love him so?” he asked tenderly.

“More than I can say,” Suzanna replied so softly that Padre Lores had to bend close to catch her words.

The friar muttered to himself as he repeated the girl’s words.

“And this young gentleman,—has he no thought for you? Does he hold his wealth and position dearer than his love for you? Time there was when men sacrificed their all for love. It seems to me ’twere easy to steal away in this broad country; to find a priest; yes, and to win a livelihood had one the courage.”

“The thought is not priestly, Padre Lores,” Suzanna exclaimed. “Would you advise a worthy son to desert his parents; to turn his back on a princely fortune; to contract a mixed marriage?”

“Indeed I would!” the friar declared emphatically. “Were I this boy, I would dare the devil himself for you! And this talk of mixed marriages,—what does it amount to? I have watched you, and I have seen you more the lady than those who so loudly proclaim themselves such. There is no place here for the cant and narrowness of Spain. This is a new land. I love it; and I have gloried in spoiling the schemes of those who try to perpetuate the injustices of Mexico and Spain within its borders."

In his excitement Padre Lores' hood had fallen about his shoulders. The moon was high enough to cast her light into the patio, and his face was boldly outlined. Suzanne's hands went to her heart as she recognized him.

"No wonder I recognized your voice," she gasped. "You are no priest at all. You are Benito Pérez!"

"What use to deny the truth?" Pérez asked. "But I beg of you, do not whisper the name again. And think not, little one, that I have tricked you. I have waited since noon for a word with you. Give over any evil thought you have toward me, for I would serve you as few men would. You are not for me,—'tis my great regret; but I am no less your servant."

"But what do you here?" Suzanna questioned nervously.

"A——matter of business," Pérez answered non-committally. "But let us talk of yourself. I overheard that bootlicking Alvarez tell his son that if he failed to wed you that he would cut him off without a cent. I see that is not news to you. But does it not strike you as strange that the father, who has ever tried for money and position, should force his son to wed you, a penniless peon?"

"I thought the boy but talked words. Now, that you state it for the truth, I am amazed. What reason can the man have?"

"Be sure he has one, and to his advantage, too," Pérez warned. "The man lives by scheming. The world allows me some sense of cleverness; but I am dull this once, or else the man is overly sharp. I would go to no little trouble to spoil any plan of his; and I swear to you that I shall have his secret. But now the guests are leaving, and you'll be looked for, little one. Go back to your friends. Remember, I am never far away. A word from you and I will come no matter the risk. And take courage; for no man is married until the priest has done with him. Your eyes are too pretty for tears. Reward me with a smile before you go.”

The personality of the bandit won her respect. She knew him for a man of action, of truth. Many far greater than she would have counted themselves fortunate to have claimed his friendship. The smile she gave him, he won from her; but of her own accord, she offered the man her hand, and Pérez bowed low over it as he brushed it with his lips.

He followed her with his eyes until she entered the house. He permitted himself a moment’s retrospection before he moved on. Suzanna stirred the best that was within him.

“Holy Mother,” he breathed half-aloud, “she is worth it. I shall leave no stone unturned to bring her happiness; and if my Lord Gutierrez does not take her to wife, it will be through no fault of mine.”

The time for sentiment this night was at an end with Pérez. Business had brought him to the hacienda; although it was business of a nefarious nature. Such as it was, the moment to busy himself with it had arrived, and he dismissed Suzanna from his thoughts. So while others slept, he toiled.

And in the morning Don Diego found that Padre Lores had disappeared; and also, sad to relate, most of the de Sola silver. Its loss so absorbed Don Diego's attention that he did not notice until hours later that his very dear friend, the Señor Alvarez was also missing. Pinned to the man's bedroom door by a heavy-handled knife was this note:

"Señor Alvarez has been called to the court of last resort.   PÉREZ."

CHAPTER XX

"It will lead to your death!"

Don Diego and Don Fernando organized their best men immediately and scoured the hills for Pérez. Nothing came of it, for the good reason that the vaqueros had no personal quarrel with the bandit. In secret, they admired, even worshiped the man. How else could he have roamed the countryside at will these many years? Pérez had foreseen that he would be harried sore for this exploit, and he had put many miles between himself and the hacienda before daybreak.

The excitement which the man left behind him threatened to delay Chiquita's wedding. Even Don Diego suggested it to her; but the girl would not listen to such an arrangement. A week was a short enough time in which to make ready; and now that two days had been lost in chasing Pérez, the time remaining had needs be taken advantage of in every way.

Don Diego repaired to Monterey at once, Don Fernando and his wife accompanying him. An orgy of buying followed. And while they were gone, things went on without a wasted moment at the hacienda. Don Fernando had loaned his friend a score of servants, captained by Ruiz. The man could be relied on to get the most out of his men.

Don Fernando, though, had noted a change in his old servitor. The man had not shown the interest in Ramon's wedding that his master had expected of him. Ruiz' face was seldom pleasant to see, but this last day or two, he had worn the look of one about to be sent to his death.

In Ruiz' mind no less a catastrophe impended. But he was between fires. A word from him and this wedding would never take place. But how could he utter that word? Death, indeed, stared at him if he did. As the days wore on, he went to bed with the firm resolve to speak to Don Fernando in the morning; but when morning came, he always found it expedient to wait until evening. And so, whatever courage he possessed failed him, and helpless, he waited for the inevitable to happen.

Miguel had seized his father's dilemma as fitting excuse for turning from his conquest of Suzanna. But although the boy made a great show of searching for his parent, it is all too true that he took exceeding care to be back at the *caserio* before sundown.

Montesoro smiled to himself as he watched the boy; glad to see his attentions to Suzanna at an end. In fact, Suzanna and Pancho laughed together over Miguel. Montesoro was playing his cards with all the skill he possessed. Day by day he saw that Suzanna leaned upon him more and more.

Ramon had made no attempt to see her since the *fiesta*. The boy was in the depths. A hurried cup of coffee in the early morning, and he was off for the day, treading lonely cañons and mountain plateaus; his thoughts as grim as the country through which he rode.

Montesoro suspected as much; but with extreme satisfaction he saw the effect of Ramon's absence on Suzanna. The boy's failure to see the girl but proved what he had told her,—that Ramon would do as his father ordered. Pancho's confidence grew. Let the boy stay away until the wedding and nothing could stop him from winning Suzanna.

Suzanna was forced to aid in the preparations for the forthcoming marriage; and each hour seemed to bring a fresh heartache, for in every conceivable way Chiquita wounded her pride. Ruiz kept away from her, and so she turned to Montesoro as her only friend.

Six days had passed without a word from Ramon. This alone told her, better than words, how foolish she had been to hope that in spite of everything he would claim her.

Every one had so much to do in the day that remained that Suzanna failed of even a kind word from Don Diego. This day, too, Chiquita went to the altar room and rehearsed the wedding ceremony. It meant agony for Suzanna. In spite of herself tears filled her eyes, and Chiquita reprimanded her. She knew what Suzanna was going through. The pity, that she was mean and small enough to take pleasure from humbling one who was impotent to turn her scorn!

Montesoro had worried through the day. He had promised himself that if Ramon did not seek Suzanna by evening that he would risk his own chance of success in an attempt to stampede the girl into marrying him at once.

Ramon did not come, so Pancho made his toss with fate. And again luck favored him, for Suzanna's pride still smarted from the hurt Chiquita had given it.

Montesoro showed a distinct aversion to words as he sat beside her in the garden. It was a peaceful night. He had brought his guitar and he strummed it softly without conscious effort. Lights glowed in the kitchen where work went on unabated this night of nights. From above came the mellow laughter of men who had dined well,—Don Diego, the Bishop of Monterey, and his three assistants.

Suzanna was glad of the man's silence; so they sat, each busy with his or her own thoughts; but ever and anon Pancho's guitar whispered its rich, sonorous music. And as it kept on without ever a lost beat, it caught up the thoughts of both of them. Its insistence seemed to hypnotize the girl. As she listened she fancied it saying, "Why be unhappy?— Why be unhappy? Life is all about you; life is good; but youth is soon lost. Come,— come before it is too late."

And as Pancho's fingers continued to dance over the strings the voice of the guitar argued its plea so persistently that Suzanna nodded her head un-

consciously. As from a distance she heard Pancho
say:

"It is as I have said, precious one; he does not
come."

Without glancing at her, he set his fingers to
moving over the strings of the guitar again. Three
or four minutes passed before he next addressed
her.

"I have had good news this day. My patrons
in Monterey have advanced me a hundred English
pounds."

He spoke disinterestedly in a monotone that
placed no inflection on his words. As he finished,
he turned to his guitar again. And thus, a sen-
tence or two at a time, did he make known his
mind. He expected no answer, nor did he wait to
receive one, and never did eagerness creep into his
voice.

The hypnosis of the thing not only caught Suzanna, but the man as well. When he laid down
his guitar and turned to her impulsively, he believed he spoke the truth, so thoroughly had he
steeped himself in his own magic.

"To-morrow at this time they will be gone," he

began. "Have you given any thought to what your life is going to be when they return?"

Suzanna answered honestly. She had seen tomorrow as the end of all things.

"They will come back, you know," Pancho went on. "Honeymoons do not last forever. That devil will take delight in keeping you as her maid. What better chance does she want to humble you continuously?—to let you see the happiness which you fancied might have been yours? She is as cruel as the Inquisition. And if you dare to resent her, what happens to you? No! No!" he exclaimed angrily. "You are not going to submit to that. You have pride; so have I. Do you think that I am going to allow you to be shamed by her? Never! I have more than enough to support us in far better style than you live in here. Say that you will be mine, Suzanna. Let me take you to Monterey. There are no blooded bulls in California. What have I to fear in the ring? I shall earn much money. Every tiniest wish of yours will be fulfilled. Look at me, my treasure, my heart, my life! I think only of you. Tell me that you love me. Let me kiss you; hold you close to my heart, for I am dying of love for you."

His appeal was more than Suzanna's love-hungry heart could withstand, and in a daze she felt herself drawn into his arms, and his lips pressed to her own.

And now the fervor of the man near ruined his chances, for his base nature flamed at Suzanna's surrender. He felt her draw away, and some warning sense of his danger coming to him, he released her reluctantly.

"Never fear, precious one, we shall humble her who has thought to humble you. Have you wedding garments?"

"Sufficient," Suzanna answered. "Don Fernando presented me with a chest on my last birthday."

"Then we shall wed to-morrow!" Pancho exclaimed determinedly. "On the very day the other wedding is to occur! There are priests aplenty to hand. Gold can arrange it. Tell me, my heart's blood, that you are willing."

Here was revenge! Poor Suzanna was only human. And what difference did it make whether she wed this man to-morrow or a month from to-morrow? No matter what Ramon's duty was, he could have found time for a word,—a last farewell with her. And then too, girls had to marry.

Many wed without hope of love; and to less personable men than this handsome *torero*. Anything was better than to stay here serving the woman who had taken Ramon from her.

Montesoro did not hurry her for an answer. He watched her face, though, and saw the emotions which crossed it, and knew that he was winning. So when Suzanna nodded her head, he was ready with suggestion.

"Speak to Don Diego at once," he begged. "I hear him in his study now. I will arrange with the priest when you return. Until you are back I will wait at the foot of the ladder beneath your window. Art bashful at speaking to your master, Suzanna?"

Suzanna smiled bravely, and moved slowly away toward the house, little aware that as she did so Ramon scaled the patio wall.

The boy had ridden untold miles that day, torn between his duty to his father and his love for Suzanna. The forfeiting of his estate he held lightly enough. Even the difference of castes did not hold him back. The love he bore his father and mother, his duty to them, the breaking of their hearts,—these were the real barriers.

Dinner time had found him miles from home.

In the last three days he had tasted but sparingly of food. His horse begged for his head that he might race over the long miles to the *caserio*. Home was the last place Ramon wanted to see. This lonely spot fitted his mood. The whippoorwills were winging over the sage already, their plaintive call no more sad than his heart.

For a full hour the boy held his position upon the rim of the mesa. Night was at hand when still decisionless, he began the long journey homeward. He held himself a coward, a weakling, for he knew that he waited now for something outside of himself to force a decision for him.

In this bitter mood he had arrived home only to find a priest waiting to confess him. The sight of the good man wrenched a groan from the boy's lips. The padre's mission here brought home what the morrow held more poignantly than aught else could.

In a blind rage, Ramon had hurled himself from the room, and rushed off to find Suzanna. He dared not ask for admission at the patio gate, so moving stealthily, he had climbed the wall and dropped safely to the ground.

Without hesitation he moved toward the ladder

which lead to Suzanna's quarters. Even now, he did not know what he would say to her; but the desire to be with her, to hear her voice and look into her eyes had swept away all other considerations. Deftly, he ascended to her room and looked for her. A glance told him she was not there.

"In the kitchen, no doubt," he muttered to himself, "wearing her fingers off for my future wife, —ha!" With an exclamation of disgust he went back to the ladder.

Montesoro confronted him as he stepped to the ground.

"Yours is rather strange conduct, señor," Pancho ground out sullenly. "I had hardly expected to see a man who is to be married in the morning, leaving the room of another woman the night before; and as the other woman happens to be my promised wife, I resent it."

Even though he was in a beastly temper, Ramon could not repress a start at the boldness with which Montesoro coupled his own name with Suzanna's.

"You are still my father's guest," the boy whipped out savagely, "albeit you are heartily unwelcome. Even so, I am hard pressed to be civil to you. But man to man, you know that you are nought to her whose name you mention."

"You are certain, eh,—señor?" Montesoro drawled sarcastically. "Permit me to suggest that you may change your mind on the morrow."

The note of confidence in his voice was too genuine to be ignored.

"Do you mean that you have tricked her into marrying you?" Ramon exclaimed.

"I mean that we will be married in the morning," Pancho shot back. "Don Diego has just given his consent."

The boy went weak all of a sudden. The desire to kill this man swept over him as a fire sweeps a forest. And Suzanna,—had she loved him so little? Ramon asked. And then his conduct this past week came back to smite him. He saw now how he had seemed to spurn her. He had brought this calamity upon himself. He was the great fool!

Could this be the end of his dreaming, Ramon asked himself. Was it possible that Suzanna had accepted this man? But why not? Montesoro was the type of man to stampede a girl. And himself, what had he done that he could expect Suzanna to wait for him? Nothing! And what could he do, even now, in the short space of time before he led Chiquita to the altar?

In a voice that he failed to recognize for his own he addressed himself to Montesoro.

"If we were two strange men, one of us would die here. To my great regret we are not. But mark this well,—if you persist in what you have told me to-night,—it will lead to your death!"

CHAPTER XXI

"PÉREZ, I NEED YOU!"

DON DIEGO unlocked the door of his study to
admit Suzanna. He showed his surprise at seeing
her.

"What is it, child?" he questioned kindly.

"I have come to ask the greatest favor a peon
girl can ask of her master," Suzanna replied
steadily.

"So?" Don Diego exclaimed. "You know full
well that I am not one to deny you, Suzanna.
Come, sit down," and Don Diego led her into his
apartment.

The girl felt a great longing to fly into the arms
of this kindly gentleman. Although he was only
her god-father, Don Diego had ever shown her more
consideration than the man whom she called father.
In the days of her childhood she had turned to him
instinctively, and her faith in his generosity and
justness had not abated since she had grown to

womanhood. So, with less trepidation than might be supposed she spoke to him now.

"Don Diego," she murmured softly, her eyes unafraid, "I want your permission to marry."

"To do what?" Señor de Sola demanded.

"To marry," Suzanna repeated.

"Well! Well!—Well!" he exclaimed, shaking his head in wonderment. "So my little Suzanna is to be married. But who is the fortunate man? Is he one of Don Fernando's vaqueros or mine?"

"He is not a vaquero, Don Diego. It is Señor Montesoro."

"Humph!" Don Diego cleared his throat, not as well pleased as he might have been. Suzanna had held a peculiar attraction for him, and he was loath to see her wed a man, who although of better social position, was one about whom he knew but little.

"You love the man?" he asked at last.

"He has been very kind to me, Don Diego."

"Well, Suzanna, it is not in my heart on this night to deny any one of my people, you least of all. I have heard no bad word of Montesoro. He seems to be a gentleman, as some members of his calling have proven themselves; for all that it is a profession given to licentiousness. I hear that he has secured the patronage of some wealthy gentlemen in Monterey. For your sake, I hope he does well. I had rather expected the man to contract a more propitious marriage. This news will come as a great surprise to all of us."

"Do I understand that you give me permission to marry him, Don Diego?" Suzanna inquired nervously.

"If it pleases you, yes. Have you thought of a day?"

"To-morrow,—if it could be arranged,—before the padres leave?"

"Send Señor Montesoro to me this evening," Don Diego answered. "I will ask the Bishop to acquiesce in the matter of the bans. And now, child, come to my arms for my own blessing."

Tears filled the girl's eyes as Don Diego released her.

"Tears of happiness," he murmured, "—they are the only tears worth while."

With a protecting arm about her, he led her to the door.

"Do not fear that you will go to your husband a penniless bride," he whispered in her ear as she bade him good-night. "Your *padrino* will see to that."

Don Diego had sent for Chiquita upon entering his study, earlier, and the girl appeared as Suzanna was leaving. Don Diego called her back.

"Here is a surprise, my daughter," he said to Chiquita. "Little Suzanna is going to be married to-morrow."

"Wha-t-t!" Chiquita gasped.

"I knew you would be surprised," Señor de Sola reiterated. "She is to become the wife of Señor Montesoro."

"Why—why—it is impossible!" Chiquita cried. She could not believe her ears. What devil's revenge was this that Pancho had contrived? She seemed about to faint. Don Diego put his arms about her, his eyes wide with surprise.

"What is it, Chiquita?" he asked. "Does this news effect you so?"

"No—no," the girl answered. "I'm overly tired. But it is a surprise, father." She spoke to Suzanna then. "Do you love the man?" she demanded.

Suzanna but looked at her and smiled. It was her moment.

"He swears that he loves me," she murmured. "That is enough. Seldom does a girl marry the man she loves."

Chiquita winced. She understood the other's meaning. A fitting retort trembled upon her tongue, but Don Diego's questioning eyes stilled it. Leaning heavily upon his arm, Chiquita implored him to lead her into his study. Suzanna knew that she was dismissed, and she bowed respectfully.

Chiquita was at some pains to turn the query in Don Diego's eyes at her conduct. This she did at last, and the good man chided her kindly for not having warned him that she had undertaken too much in arranging for her wedding in such a brief time.

"I sent for you, Chiquita," he said finally, "to have a last minute or two alone with you before you pass from my care to your husband's. You know full well how happy you have made me by accepting Ramon. Already you have had substantial proof of my gratitude; but I hold that what I have done is no proper gift. I have here, however, that which I hold dearest of all my possessions. It is my wish, my daughter, to present it to you now."

Don Diego unlocked his desk and withdrew a

small, iron-bound casket. Chiquita's breath came unevenly as she watched him. She divined the contents of this chest.

Señor de Sola opened it and bid her look. An array of sparkling jewels greeted her eyes. The girl had often heard of the de Sola heirlooms, but she had never put eyes to them until now.

Don Diego thrilled at the sound of the glad cry which escaped Chiquita. Impulsively he put his hand into the casket and brought forth a magnificent string of lustrous pearls. With the grace of a courtier, he dropped them about her shoulders.

"My daughter," murmured huskily, his voice heavy with emotion, "these are the most prized possessions of our family. Kings and queens have worn these jewels; they are fit only for kings and queens. And because you are a queen,—the queen of my heart, I bestow them on you, with no other wish than that you may be as happy as those others who have worn them with such pride and honor. They are yours, my daughter,—my wedding gift to you and Ramon."

Not until she had fondled each separate jewel would Chiquita consent to their being placed into the vault for the night. So great was her joy in this wonderful gift that she quite forgot Montesoro for the minute. Had she been so minded, Chiquita could have read her own character from this fact. She was an individualist. She took; but she never gave.

An hour later, however, thought of the man did come to her, and she cursed him for shaming her by marrying a peon beneath her very nose. And yet so perverse was her nature that her infatuation for the man but grew, in that he could be so superbly cruel to her.

She gave no thought to the man she was to wed within a few hours. In fairness, let it be said, Ramon gave no thought to her. He had returned to the waiting padre, and made his pre-nuptial confession. But it was significant of how little weight the customs of the Church had with him, that once finished with the priest, he went in search of Guara, the Indian, and sent him off with a note post-haste to no other than the outlaw, Pérez.

The fact that in his need of an ally he should be forced to turn to one who roamed the country with a price on his head made him smile mirthlessly. It was a grim indictment of his fellow men; but who else would dare what he asked of Pérez?

The letter which Ramon handed to Guara, read:

"Pérez, I need you. Unless you can contrive to prevent it, Suzanna will be married to-morrow morning to Montesoro. It is too late for argument. No matter what the danger, I beg you to carry her off. I guarantee you with my life that you shall not come to harm.
My hand on it,
RAMON GUTIERREZ."

"I do not know where you will find the man, Guara," the boy said to the Indian. "He is somewhere in the Santa Cruz hills. Take a lead horse with you; drive them to the limit. There is no danger for you in this, except you fail me. The night is clear: you know the trails well. Go!—And by the blood of your fathers, Guara, swear to me that you will find him."

CHAPTER XXII

THE GROOM TAKES HIS PLACE

MORNING dawned without the Indian having returned. Ramon tramped his room impatiently. In two hours his father would be coming for him. What had happened to Guara? Had his fear of Pérez proven greater than his devotion to his master's son? Glancing from his window, Ramon saw that already the carriage in which he and Chiquita were to ride away had drawn up before Don Diego's house, its wheels and body covered with flowers. The patios of his own home were a riot of color as servants and guests moved about in holiday splendor.

The boy had his coffee served to him in his room. Fifteen minutes later his father sent word that it was time to dress. Ramon stole to the roof of the house and swept the horizon for sight of Guara as soon as the servant had left. The road was dotted with many traveling hitherward; but the pace at which they moved was proof enough that the Indian was not among them.

Despairing, his brain dulled to what went on about him, he stumbled downstairs to his room. His father's barber awaited him. Mechanically, Ramon permitted the man to shave him. The barber had not left before another servant arrived to lay out his wedding garments, and to help his young master don them.

The boy's indifference hindered the man, and before the dressing was accomplished Ramon's father came in. Don Fernando was fully attired for the wedding, and he raised his eyebrows at his son's apparent tardiness.

"We have but a quarter of an hour," he warned. "Your mother is waiting already."

Ramon nodded his head silently.

"Join us as soon as you can, then," his father ordered. "Everything has been attended to."

Ramon's thoughts as he surveyed himself in his mirror were the bitterest of his life. In his resplendent clothes of velvet and doeskin, he was a handsome figure. Somehow the scowl on his face but enhanced the quality of his strong features.

The servant begged him to come to the window

for a glimpse of the bridal procession which was forming in Don Diego's patio. Ramon glared at the man for his trouble. Now, that it was too late, the boy could have leaped from that window and dashed for the distant hills.

Trapped, his heart dead within him, he joined his parents. A cry broke from the crowd as they stepped from the house. It was for Ramon, and the boy bowed in recognition. Then with full regard for the dignity of the occasion, Don Fernando led the way to Don Diego's mansion.

Señor de Sola met them and escorted them into his study. He noted the paleness of Ramon's face.

"My son," he whispered to him. "Let me get you a nip of the best brandy in California. This day is ever one of terror for a man. Come." And placing his arm through the boy's, he led him away, vouchsafing a smile to Don Fernando and Doña Luz.

Every step that Ramon took was one of fear. He refused to think what he would do if he should encounter Suzanna. The corridors were filled with hurrying servants. Only a miracle could prevent their meeting. And yet, they did not, for at that very moment Suzanna was donning her own wedding dress.

By the time that Don Diego and Ramon returned to the study it was time for the marriage to occur. Kissing his mother, the boy permitted himself to be led to his position before the chancel in the chapel.

Barely had he taken his place when the Bishop and his assistants appeared. Ramon eyed them stonily as they mounted the altar steps. The Bishop began the mass, the audience singing the responses; but Ramon gave no heed to the multitude or its whispered comments. Solemn, erect, he stood as a man stands before a firing squad. But once did he smile, and it was his mother who won it from him as she took her position on the opposite side of the chancel. There was such sadness in his eyes that Doña Luz' heart bled for him. She fancied she knew the sacrifice this son of hers made.

"Dominus vobiscum," the Bishop droned. And then through the door at Ramon's side came his father. Behind him the boy caught a glimpse of the wedding procession. Leading it came Chiquita on the arm of Don Diego; the man proud, stately.

Chiquita, her head slightly bowed, a suspicious

pinkness in her olive tinted cheeks, was almost incomparably beautiful. Her wedding gown, a wondrous garment of satin and rare lace, flared widely at the bottom, and as she walked her red slippers peeped out cautiously. Draped about her shoulders clung a mantilla of purest silver thread. A jeweled comb sparkled in her midnight hair. The mantilla hung from this ornament in her hair, and as she turned her head both comb and mantilla glistened in the sunlight.

Ramon had to admit that she was beautiful,— but hers was the beauty that kills.

A procession of children followed in the bridal train, casting flowers at the bride and her attend- ants, and making a veritable pathway of blossoms upon which the bride and groom were to tread as they left the chapel.

The last of the children entered, and Ramon saw his bride take her place opposite him. Turn- ing his eyes away, that she might not read his thoughts, he stared through the open door at the flower strewn path. And as he continued to gaze into the empty patio, he saw Montesoro and Suz- anna move across the garden toward a temporary altar which had been hurriedly arranged for their marriage.

Suzanna's olive tinted cheeks were pale; but she was magnificent in her wedding garments as head erect she walked beside the man whom she was about to wed. Never once did she look to the right or left, but continued with steady step toward the altar.

Montesoro was clad in fitting raiment, and although he hovered near Suzanna protectingly, he shot a hurried glance toward the chapel, dreading some last minute interference with his plans.

Ramon's blood froze in his veins as he beheld the two of them. What had happened to Guara? Had the Indian's courage failed him? Surely he had not found Pérez, or else the man would have come. Another ten minutes and no power on earth could stop Suzanna from marrying the man beside her.

A look of horror crossed the boy's face. Terror came into his eyes. And then as he watched, he saw another figure follow them, a man in dashing raiment. Something familiar about the swagger of him struck Ramon. His lips moved inarticulately as he strained his eyes for a better look at the man's face.   And then, like a flash, the boy's eyes snapped.

His blood warmed again.   He wanted to cry out, to shout with ecstacy, for here was help.   Let Montesoro and the others do their worst, they dealt with a man now.

"Por Dios!" he mumbled.   "I knew he would not fail me.   It's Pérez, himself!"

CHAPTER XXIII

"THE WAY IS OPEN!"

GUARA had not found Pérez. The man had
come unsummoned to the *caserio*. He had timed
his arrival well, and for once he entered by the
gate. Neither Pancho or Suzanna had seen him
waiting for them to cross to the altar. In fact, they
did not become aware of his presence until he addressed them.

Montesoro's hand went to his sword as he recognized the bandit. Pérez ignored him, and turning to Suzanna he said:

"I am late,—as usual; but not too late—and as
I have come all the way from Monterey since sunrise, perhaps you will forgive my tardiness."

Suzanna had no ready answer, so great a shock
had his appearance given her. Pérez saw her confusion.

"You did not send for me, as I suggested," he
ran on, "but that prize fool, Miguel, unwittingly
served as your messenger."

The man spoke in riddles. But he was not one to risk his neck for the thrill of it.

"Miguel?" Suzanna questioned, hoping to discover what it was that Pérez was trying to say. "Have you taken him prisoner, too."

The man bowed as he answered.

"Miguel is also a guest of mine," he replied ironically. "Or rather I might say that I have been their guest; inasmuch as the entertainment has taken place within the walls of Señor Alvarez's own home. But no matter,—as a companion, the father has proven a distinct disappointment; his sense of humor is negligible. But allow me to say, Señorita, that I have succeeded in finding out why friend Alvarez was so exceedingly anxious to have his son wed you."

Pancho had stood being brushed aside as long as he could bear it. With a clicking of syllables he said to Pérez:

"You choose an ill time for your gossip. You will find the wedding presents arrayed in Don Diego's study."

"So-o-o?" Pérez inquired with rising inflection, a dreadful whine in his voice. "Think you that I am always bent on business? I have my moments, man. The time is short; allow me to finish."

"Not if it is only idle gossip which you have to retail!"

Pérez smiled to himself.

"I will leave that to your judgment, Señor," he replied. "Suzanna," he began again, "on the word of a lawyer, I can assure you that you have been most grievously sinned against."

Suzanna smiled enigmatically, at a loss to understand the man.

"On unimpeachable authority, believe me, I say to you that you are the real Chiquita de Sola. The girl, who stands inside that chapel door about to wed young Gutierrez, is a peon,—the daughter of Ruiz, the peon!"

Suzanna's hand leaped to her mouth.

"Wha-t-t-t!" she cried, her body trembling. Surely this man was mad. In fear, she stepped nearer to Pancho, and sent an appealing glance at him. But Montesoro was speechless. Was this girl to be snatched away from him at the very altar?

"I repeat myself," Pérez went on, "you are Don

Diego's daughter! I suspect that this man has known it for some time."

"Your suspicions are in keeping with the rest of your weird tale," Montesoro cried angrily. "Enough of your witless chatter! Ramon saved you once; I doubt if he could accomplish it were I to raise my voice now."

Pérez made no reply until he had stared the man down.

"There is truth in your surmise," he said at last. "But you will not cry out against me, señor,—I am quite certain of that. And as for witless chatter,— a man does not speak witlessly when hot irons are caressing the soles of his feet. Believe me, Señor Alvarez never spoke more to the point. Ruiz went to him with his secret. Here I have the statement of friend Alvarez!"

Tersely then did Pérez acquaint Suzanna with the truth. No wonder there had always been a warm affection in her heart for Don Diego; it was the natural affinity of a daughter for her father.

Weak, dazed, Suzanna leaned against the altar for support. How would her father receive this news And Don Fernando,—and Ramon?— would he scorn her now? And then her heart al-

most stopped beating. The marriage! No doubt
but what the Bishop was pronouncing Chiquita
man and wife this very instant. Pérez had said
that he was not too late; but he was! What good
could come of his news now? The document he
had given her burned her fingers.

The girl's brain reeled and her power to think
left her. She heard a strange voice, which she
barely recognized for Montesoro's, saying:

"It's a story-book tale that you tell. You will
have to prove it! And you have not named *your*
price, either."

Pérez started to reply, but Suzanna stopped him.
Turning to Pancho she asked:

"Does it not make you happy to know the truth?"

"More than I can say,—if it is the truth," Montesoro muttered. "But the thought of losing you is
maddening."

"I have not said that I would not marry you,"
Suzanna answered slowly.

"But *I* say that you shall not marry him!" a
voice boomed behind her. "You are mine, and no
man shall take you from me!"

That voice! Suzanna put out her hand un-
steadily.

"Ramon!" she whispered. "My Ramon——"

"At last," he said to her. "God bless you, Pérez," he exclaimed as he turned to the bandit. "Have you a horse?"

"Outside the gate,—a white stallion. The crowd is coming!"

Ramon reached for Suzanna, and as he did so, Pancho's sword flashed.

"You'll not run so fast!" he cried aloud.

The boy was caught without hope of defending himself. Suzanna screamed as she saw the steel blade reach for Ramon's throat. And then through the air another blade whistled; the swish of it ending in a groan as Montesoro sank to the ground, pierced to the heart.

"Go!" Pérez commanded. "The way is open!"

CHAPTER XXIV

"WHITHER DO WE GO?"

RAMON had stood at the chancel, waiting, until his hands had shaken, for some sign of action on the part of Pérez. Helplessly he had fought the excitement raging within him. The Bishop had read the *Pater Noster;* another minute or two and the mass would be over; the wedding would be consummated. Something in Ramon had snapped, then. Time and place, parents, betrothed, custom, traditions,— everything was swept away in the flood of emotion which had engulfed him. The decision he had despaired of ever reaching, had given him strength. Let the cost be what it might, Chiquita de Sola could be no bride of his! Without pausing to calculate his chances of success, he had leaped through the door and rushed to Suzanna's side.

The crowd had murmured at his unceremonious exit. Don Fernando and Don Diego exchanged a wondering glance, but even now they had no suspicion of what went forward in the patio; and it was not until the sound of angry voices arose that Ramon's father stepped to the door. His eye took in the scene at a glance,—Montesoro lying dead at the foot of the altar; Pérez, sword in hand standing above him; Ramon running for the gate, Suzanna in his arms.

"Hold! Hold!" He cried aloud. "Stop them!"

The crowd in the chapel was thrown into a panic. Men, who had been friends but a moment before, fought each other to gain access to the garden.

Don Fernando had drawn his sword on seeing no one arise to bar the way to Ramon's escape. The portly man called again as he ran after them; but as the crowd poured into the garden, Ramon lifted Suzanna onto the horse's back and swung into the saddle in front of her.

"Stop! Stop him!" Don Fernando shouted, but the cry was in vain; Ramon and Suzanna dashed away.

The boy's father turned to his men, who surrounded him. "Pursue them!" he ordered.

Horses were needed first, before this could be done, and minutes must elapse before they could be saddled. Ramon was heading for the hills to the west. In a few minutes, he was far enough away from the *caserio* to permit those who watched to follow him with their eyes.

“He *is* pursued!” some one cried.

And true enough, a long-striding black horse had turned from the road and was leaping after the fugitives.

“That horse,” Don Fernando exclaimed,—“his gait is familiar!”

“ ’Tis Guara,” Ruiz answered. “I recognize the horse he rides.”

“He bids fair to overtake them. But to your horses, men. And look to it you are quick about it!”

Ramon and Suzanna had passed from sight by now, Guara riding close.

Another mile and the Indian caught up with them. The boy had seen that they were followed, and that their pursuer must overtake them.

Suzanna pointed to him in alarm.

“Never fear!” Ramon cried. “By my life I swear they shall not take you from me.”

That it was Guara who followed them, caused the boy to wonder; but be he friend or foe, Ramon vowed that the Indian should not turn him back.

Sword in hand, he swung to the ground and faced the man.

The Indian shook his head at sight of the boy's drawn sword.

"Do you mean that you come as a friend?" Ramon questioned. "Didn't my father order you to bring us back?"

"I have not seen your father. I was returning to the *Caserio* when I saw you gallop off. Pérez—he came, I see," Guara smiled, pointing to the outlaw's horse. "He was in Monterey; I ride one horse to death trying to find him."

"Your reward shall not be forgotten, Guara."

"This black mare is for her," the man grinned, nodding toward Suzanna. "She is fresh. Hurry! Many men come soon."

Ramon's only plan so far had been to get away from the *caserio*. He knew the hill trails to the west. One of them led to Monterey. If they were fortunate enough to reach there, they could find a haven of refuge; but the way was overly long for Suzanna.

The Indian seemed to sense the boy's indecision as he wheeled his horse ahead of Suzanna's mare. With cunning quite equal to a white man's, Guara said pointedly: "The lower trail leads to San Carmelo."

Ramon smiled. Here was the plan he had lacked! With a wave of his hand to the Indian, the boy gave his horse its head and he and Suzanna drew rapidly away.

It was forty miles to San Carmelo. The pace began to tell on the girl. "Whither do we go?" she cried as they swept down into a rocky cañon.

"To the Mission San Carlos de Carmelo," Ramon flung back at her without ever slacking the speed at which they rode.

San Carlos de Carmelo,—the Mission! Suzanna smiled bravely to herself. What mattered this torturing saddle now?

She thought of Pérez as she rode, and of the sacrifice the man had made for her, for surely he had been captured that they might ride free. The man had proven himself a true friend; and in spite of all his failings, Suzanna found him worthy of her respect.

The bandit had been captured as she surmised. Indeed, he had made no attempt to escape; nor did he resist when Don Diego ordered him bound.

Ramon's act was a cruel blow to Señor de Sola.

He is to be pardoned for venting his wrath on Pérez. The bandit was the only one of the guilty ones to hand, and Don Diego had also the matter of his silver against the man.

Chiquita had been carried away in a faint from Montesoro's side. It was to the dead man that Don Diego pointed as he addressed the bound bandit.

"You have not the effrontery to deny that you killed him, I hope?"

"I killed him," Pérez answered.

"You turn from robber to murderer with surprising ease," Don Diego stormed. "And only with your connivance did yonder couple escape. I suppose you do not deny that, either."

"I do not. As men go, I have never been known as a liar."

"But are you so calloused as to offer no excuse for your conduct?"

"I have never been one for excuses, most noble sir. Reason, now, I have; but excuse——? No! And although I well may not be alive to hear you say it, the day will come when you will admit that I have done you greater service this day than has any man in your time."

"Well, give it a name, then!" Don Diego exclaimed.

"That shall remain for other lips than mine. But here are your men with horses; although I warn you, you but waste your time in attempting to follow that fleeing pair. My men are in those hills to the west; if they allow you to pass, it will be because they know you come too late to matter."

CHAPTER XXV

ALONE AT LAST

SUZANNA and Ramon did not suspect that unseen friends guarded their escape. The boy urged the horses on whenever the going permitted, and before noon they caught their first glimpse of the Mission. Even viewed from a distance, San Carlos de Carmelo breathed a sense of rest and security. A wide valley, mostly cultivated meadow land, stretched between the Mission and the spot where Ramon and Suzanna sood for a brief moment. They felt safe now, for they could win to the Mission long before any pursuer could descend from the hills in back of them.

Ramon had said no word of love to the girl, and Suzanna, catching his eye, gazed from him to the Mission, a silent question on her lips. The boy failed to read her thought, so Suzanna voiced her words.

"You have not asked me to marry you, Ramon," she said with downcast eyes.

"Better far to marry and ask afterward, when irate fathers are rushing hither to stop us," the boy answered gayly.   But for all his words, he forced his horse alongside Suzanna's and catching her around the waist lifted her into his arms.   "Art hungry for a word of love from me, little one?" he whispered.   "Think you that I had forgotten? Come, place your arms about me, and let me see you smile as my lips touch yours.   The past is in back of us; and as long as we have each other, how matters it what else the future holds?"

Suzanna was tempted to tell him the truth concerning herself, but the happiness of knowing that this man loved her and was willing to marry her believing her to be a peon, was so great that she could not destroy it now.   And so, her eyes closed, she delivered her lips to him.   The wine of youth coursed through her body as her flesh met his. Yesterday was forgotten; ahead of her beckoned sunlit days at his side.   Her spirit seemed to surge up and take wings, and as a bird that has newly found its freedom, her being soared to the heights. Dimly then, from a distance, she heard Ramon's cautioning voice, and felt herself placed in her saddle again.

Neither spoke as they rode; a word would have broken the spell which held that beautiful valley and themselves prisoners. In silence, then, did they dismount before the Mission. A thin little wisp of a man, clad in the robes of the Franciscans, came out to meet them as they ascended the stone steps.

" 'Tis easy to see, my children, what brings you here," the little padre said to them.

A smile from Suzanna rewarded him.

"It is as you have surmised," Ramon declared. "It is our wish that you join us in marriage, holy father."

"But, my children, you come without witnesses, —though that is readily remedied; but the bans,— have your names been read?"

Ramon gulped. Dumbly he looked at Suzanna. Had they been fools not to think of this? As he looked at her, he saw Suzanna's lips move.

"They have, good padre," she said. "Don Ramon Gutierrez, son of Don Fernando Gutierrez; and—Chiquita de Sola, the daughter of Don Diego de Sola."

"No, no!" Ramon begged.

The Franciscan looked from one to the other as

these confusing statements greeted his ears. The names the girl had uttered were well known to him by hearsay.

"It is the truth," Suzanna reiterated bravely. "I am Chiquita de Sola. Our names were read in Monterey by the Bishop himself."

Ramon, still dumfounded, and only wondering what had caused this madness in Suzanna, took her in his arms and endeavored to calm her.

"No, Ramon!" Suzanna cried, forcing him away from her as she sought for the paper Pérez had given her. "I wanted to keep this surprise for you until we were married; but since it is necessary that the secret be told now, read this."

The boy could but stare at her as he and the priest finished reading Alvarez' statement.

"This is an honest document," the padre announced gravely. "Señor Alvarez is our notary. I recognize his signature. If you are still of a mind to wed, I will call the witnesses."

Ramon's answer was to open his arms and take Suzanna into them, her tears of happiness wetting his cheek.

And so, in the Mission San Carlos de Carmelo, they were wed; and none too soon, for barely had the ceremony ended when a dozen horsemen flung themselves into the church, Don Fernando at their head. His face was livid with rage as he advanced to the chancel.   In his hand he carried a long rawhide quirt, and as he realized that he came too late, he raised the quirt angrily and sent it hissing through the air at his son.

The Franciscan divined his intention too late to stop him, but even so he was in time to warn Ramon, but as the boy stepped backward, the lash struck Suzanna a cutting blow.

"You are in the house of God!" the padre exclaimed. "I ask judgment on you!"

The whip fell from Don Fernando's hand as he sank to his knees. "I beg forgiveness for the blow," he groaned. "I was beside myself. My son has denied me my dearest wish; he has violated a canon of our family that forever debars him from handing down to posterity an ancient and honorable name."

A great sob burst from his quivering lips as he bowed his head at his own shame and his son's.

"You are mistaken," the little padre told him. "Your son has not married a peon. His wife is of blood as noble as his own.   Dismiss your men and come into the sacristy with me."

Don Fernando waited for Don Diego to join him, and together they followed the priest behind the altar.

What need to relate what went on between them when they were closeted together? Anger gave way to wonder, and grief to happiness. Pérez' words came back to Don Diego. Truly, the man had not oversaid himself. He had done such service as few would dare.

"They shall go to my house at once," Don Diego exclaimed, referring to Ramon and his bride. "We shall have a second wedding. And when they return from their wedding trip they shall occupy the very rooms to which I led Suzanna's mother."

"But my son is to manage *my* estate," Don Fernando warned. "My house shall be his!"

"Perhaps it were well to allow the young man to decide," the priest said wisely. "Remember, he is no longer a boy."

They returned then, to the church proper; but Ramon and Suzanna, as she still chose to be called, had long since stolen away, and even then were racing their horses along the wide, wind swept beach beside the Pacific. They were alone at last; off to spend their honeymoon as lovers have ever wanted to spend it,—in peace and quiet. So there where the waves of the broad ocean break so gently upon the white sands of Carmel, let us leave them, knowing that through trial and misfortune they had come to such happiness as few attain.

THE END

9 781590 774120